Lady Shadow

Children of the Goddess, Volume 4

Prudence MacLeod

Published by Prudence MacLeod, 2024.

LADY SHADOW

First edition. January 13, 2024.

Copyright © 2024 Prudence MacLeod.

ISBN: 978-1927478493

Written by Prudence MacLeod.

Lady Shadow

by

Prudence MacLeod

Book four in the Children of the Goddess series.

Mistake

Everyone makes mistakes. Even a goddess can make a mistake. Giving things a second thought, Moragah wondered if she'd given Lady Justice too much power. Secretly, Moragah gave a little push to help Justice remain human. She hoped it would be enough, as a frightened voice in a distant city called out to be heard.

Stupid Mistake

C urled up in her favorite chair, dressed in her PJs, Lexa Condon sighed with contentment. Lovingly, she opened her book and dove into the world of adventure, leaving the stress filled world, and the past due rent, behind. Hours later she slowly withdrew her attention from the pages. Loud, shouting voices from the next apartment penetrated her awareness.

The Browns were such a quiet couple, she had never heard them raise their voices. Frowning, Lexa pressed her ear to the wall. "Goddammit, Bill, keep your voice down," shouted a male voice.

"Keep my voice down? For Christ's sake, Frank, this is our own government doing this."

"I know. So what?"

"So what? You knew? How long have you known?"

"I've always known. You're such a naive fool, Bill."

"Well, we have to do something, tell somebody."

"No, we don't." There was a soft popping sound, a woman screamed, another popping sound, and then silence.

Not sure what had happened, Lexa did something completely stupid. She went next door and knocked softly. "Hey folks, is everybody all right in there?"

The door flew open, her arm was seized, and she was yanked into the room.

"Hey, what the hell?" she demanded as the door was shut behind her. A man she had never seen before raised a gun with a silencer on it.

He shot her. Blood spurted from her head and the world vanished as she fell to the floor.

Pain and confusion entered Lexa's awareness first as she began to regain consciousness. Her vision was blurry, but after a quick groping search she found her glasses. Settling them on her face she was suddenly confronted by the horror of her situation. She was in an apartment with two dead bodies. Lexa struggled to her feet, made it to the door then opened it a crack. The hallway was empty. She quickly slipped out and closed the door behind her.

A few swift steps found her back inside her own apartment with the door locked. Only then did she raise a hand to her aching head. It came away covered in blood. The sight in her hall mirror shocked her and she nearly fainted. Her hair was matted with dried blood and there was a gash on her skull. It burned like hellfire.

Lexa tried to clean herself up, but it hurt too much and she gave up, called a cab, and went to the hospital. She told them she had fallen and hit her head on the coffee table. "That looks like a gunshot wound," said the doctor, as he gave her an injection to kill the pain. "I have to report this to the police." Lexa nodded, then closed her eyes. She didn't really care anymore; she just wanted the pain to go away.

They shaved part of her head then dressed the wound. A nurse tried to get the blood out of the rest of her hair. It took a while, but she managed it. By the time she was finished, the police had arrived. They questioned Lexa about what happened, and she told them the truth. They left her there in the hospital room and went to investigate her claim. The officers found the bodies exactly as she described and radioed in about the homicide.

A stern faced man sat alone in his hotel room, listening to a police radio. Within moments his phone rang. "There's a witness at the hospital. Lexa Condon. Get your mess cleaned up." He thumbed it off and returned to his car.

Lexa was starting to get her mind clear. She buzzed for the nurse just as a new doctor entered the room. She recognized him instantly, and he recognized her. She threw a pillow at him and rolled off the bed. It was enough of a distraction and his shot missed.

"What the hell..." The nurse who'd just entered got no further as he turned and shot her. She fell to the floor, but an orderly had seen into the room. He shouted as he tried to drag the nurse out of the line of fire. "Gun. Call security!" Without a second's hesitation the gunman threw a chair through the window and exited down the fire escape. He was gone before security could reach the scene. Lexa lay cowering under the bed, trembling in terror.

A short while later, Lexa was in a secure room with police guards posted at the door. They'd had to sedate her, but she wasn't quite asleep. She could hear the guards talking.

"What do you think, Jim?"

"This is all way over my head. I overheard the chief and the commissioner talking. Turns out those two bodies were CIA spooks. The commissioner thinks this was an in-house clean up operation."

"And this poor gal stumbled into the middle of it. Shit. I don't care much for her chances if a professional spook is after her."

"Yeah. I just hope I'm not on shift when it happens."

Lexa covered her ears and tried to pull the blanket over her head. Curled up in the fetal position, she trembled in fear. "It's not fair," she whispered to herself. In her beloved books, the heroine would rise from the ground, hurling lightning and death at the evil ones. She would walk through them, cutting them down like a scythe through a field of grain. She would destroy them utterly, find out who had sent them, and then take out the evil behind the evil. But she was no heroine; she was Lexa, the waitress who had lost her job because she refused to have sex with the cafe owner.

Never one who believed in god, Lexa had always preferred the heroes in her books to the rituals of religion, she prayed anyway. "Okay, there are thousands of gods being worshiped every day. This prayer is for any god out there who is listening. If you're really there, prove it. Help me." Nothing happened and she began to weep softly, her mind still fogged with the drug. It took her a moment to realize she was no longer alone in the room.

Trying to shake the cobwebs from her mind, Lexa peeked fearfully over the blanket. The room appeared to be empty, but she was aware of another presence. "Where are you?" she asked softly.

"I am everywhere," replied a warm gentle voice. It seemed to be amused.

"What are you?"

"You called for a god, did you not? I am Moragah, and I've answered your call. I did not immediately claim you as I waited to see if another more familiar to you would make that claim. They haven't, so I'm here. What would you have of me?"

"Wow, those pain meds were way better than I thought. Now I'm hallucinating."

"Perhaps we should start again. May I touch you?"

"What? Oh, okay I guess." Suddenly Lexa was aware of that vast presence surrounding her, relieving her pain and fear, clearing her mind. "Oh, wow," she said aloud, then whispered. "Oops, sorry. Don't want to upset the guards."

"The guards cannot hear us, nor can the man who hunts you, find you. I've taken you between worlds and time. You can speak freely here."

"Cool."

"You still believe you are hallucinating."

"Oh yeah, this is so cool. I can see everything even without my glasses."

Lexa felt the mirth in the voice as she was bathed in warm loving feelings. "All right, Lexa. Let's work with that. Tell me why you called."

"But you already know. You said there was a man hunting me, so you know what happened."

"Oh yes, but what I truly do not know is why you called. Even though you don't believe in gods, you called out. Why? What do you want a god to do for you?"

"Protect me."

"Truly, is that all you want?"

"Well..."

"You don't trust." The warmth and love Lexa felt from this vast being had her floating in bliss. She had no fear and no other desire except to be there. "You understand that for every action there is an equal reaction. You fear what I might want in return. Very well, perhaps it will be better if I go first.

"Lexa, there is a darkness falling over this country, this world. The forces of darkness grow stronger in spite of efforts to oppose them. The killing of your neighbors is just one example.

"I want you to fight the darkness. I want you to search out those who control and direct the minions of darkness."

"Me? Oh no, I'm just a girl, and not a very brave one at that."

"I know. I know you would rather hide away, but I ask you, what would the heroines of your stories do?"

"Ha, they would fight for you. Why don't you create one of them to be your hunter."

"That's the idea. That's why I answered your call. If you choose to take on this task for me I will give you the tools to accomplish the task."

"Seriously? You'd give me super powers? You're the best hallucination ever, Moragah. Which powers would you give me?"

"You would have the instincts of a wild animal. You'd know when danger approached, or when your prey was near. You would be stronger than ten men. When threatened or in great need you would be able to move so fast that the human eye could not follow, and this speed will enhance your strength. You'd be able to hear at great distance by focusing on whatever you wanted to hear. Your injuries would heal almost immediately. These are the basics that all my priestesses have.

"Above that, each priestess has certain abilities that are her own. Penny is absolutely tireless and can move about a city like a bird of prey. Kara controls fire, creates and controls it with her mind. Tasha can hide in plain sight, appearing and disappearing at will. Get the idea?"

"Okay, so what would be my special talent?"

"Hmm, Lexa, you have a powerful and vivid imagination. For you, I think the power of illusion."

"You mean like a magician?"

"That and much more. By focusing your will on an individual or group, they would see only what you wanted them to see, to hear only what you wished them to hear."

"So, I could make a guy think I was the most beautiful woman in the world?"

"If that was your wish, yes."

"Okay, now I know there's a catch," sighed Lexa, still basking in the glow of Moragah's loving energy.

"Ah yes, the catch. When I create a priestess I am forever a part of her, always within her and her awareness, sharing experiences with her. I try to guide her and protect her, but the life of a priestess is a life of danger. Not all survive it. Also, each day at sunrise the priestess greets me with a short blessing. Watch now and I'll show you. This first one is Penny."

Lexa felt Moragah's pride in the tall blonde as she watched the girl race across the rooftops of a city. She gasped at the long falls and tumbles the fierce looking warrior took. She gulped as the woman tore into a group of armed men and took them down with ease. Next she saw the woman stand beside another and call a greeting to Moragah as they faced the rising sun.

The next was a small girl and Moragah showed a mother's pride as the diminutive warrior raced at a street gang war. Lexa gasped as the girl threw a wall of flames into the battle zone then ran into it. She reappeared moments later carrying an injured child in her arms. She walked through the fire, but it did not burn her. Later she greeted Moragah at sunrise just as the taller blonde had done.

"The first was Penny," said Moragah. "The second was Kara. Now for Tasha."

Lexa saw a dark girl step out of the shadows. She was exquisitely beautiful, but her eyes were cold, so cold. She stepped out of a wall, seized a man with a gun, broke his neck and let the body fall. "Justice is served," she said as she disappeared back into the wall. Later she appeared before some sort of altar, surrounded by soldiers. "For Moragah, for Justice."

"Wow," said Lexa. "They're amazing. You want me to be like them? I could never be like them, could I?"

"Yes, you can. That's what I want for you, Lexa. Each deals with injustice in their own way wherever they find it. For you it would be different. You would be searching for the ones who direct the injustice, the chaos of darkness. Like Penny and Kara you would battle whatever crossed your path, but like Tasha, you would be always searching, pulling the weeds of the human garden."

"She looked so cold, like she had no feelings at all."

"Tasha has feelings, Lexa, but when the time of battle is on her she goes cold so she can do what must be done. It would be the same for you."

"Do you really think I could be like them?"

"Yes, but it will be difficult for you at first. I would prefer to have one of them guide you until you're comfortable with your new abilities. However, this won't be possible. So, what'll it be, Lexa? Will you join me on the great quest, the grand adventure, or shall I put you back where I found you?"

"Okay, sure, I'll do it. Make me a super hero."

"You still don't believe," said Moragah, a hint of mirth in her voice. "You soon will. Brace yourself, this part is extremely painful, but only lasts a second. Ready?"

"Ready," was the dreamy reply.

"You're not, but it has to happen. Lexa, I am deeply sorry for this."

Suddenly every cell in her body felt like it had burst into hellfire. A soul searing scream burst from her lips and the illusion of a dream was gone. Even as the two guards burst into the room with guns drawn, Lexa felt Moragah healing and soothing her wounds. Lexa sat up in the bed, gasping and trying to regain control. "Whoa, fellas, easy. Nightmare. Bad dream. Bad drugs. Sorry."

A nurse had also hurried to the room. "I'm so sorry," she said. "Sometimes the drugs can induce nightmares. Easy now, breathe deeply. I'll call the doctor and get a different prescription for you."

"No, don't bother," replied Lexa. "That stuff just makes my brain foggy. Got anything to read? That usually calms my nerves."

"I'll get you something," said the nurse, as she hurried away. The two guards had satisfied themselves that all was well and returned to their station outside the door.

"Holy smokes. That wasn't an hallucination; it was real. You're real, Moragah."

"Yes, my skeptical priestess."

"And I really have super powers?"

"You do. The ones we discussed and a few more for you to discover on your own."

"Okay, so how can I test them?"

"Pinch the bed frame."

She did and the metal buckled under her touch. "Wow. Okay, I'm going to need some practice before I get too crazy. So, what do I do now?"

"Whatever you want to do, Lexa. The task is in your hands now."

"I think I'll stay right here and play along for a while. They may send someone else after me. I could catch them and learn something useful from them, couldn't I?"

"Yes, that is a sound plan."

"Then that's what I'll do." At that point the nurse returned with a romance novel for her. Lexa thanked her then dove into the story.

The next morning a perplexed doctor released Lexa from hospital. Her scalp wound was completely healed and the hair was already starting to grow back. She'd have a scar, but once the hair grew in no one would ever see it. She'd refused protective custody, so a policeman drove her home and promised they would keep an eye on her.

Lexa noticed the bloody handprint on the door and inside the apartment on the wall. That was going to be hard to clean off. She started to cry when she finally saw her reflection in the mirror. There was a scar on her scalp and the hair had been shaved at an odd angle.

Drying her tears she found a scarf and tied it around her head, hiding the hair and restoring her sense of self. Suddenly she remembered. She hurried to the window and raised her arms high.

"Lady Moragah, I'm so sorry. The sun is up, and I forgot. Wait, a blessing. Hmmm, Moragah, I thank you for this new day to enjoy and for saving my life. May your name ever be revered and blessed." She lowered her arms and turned away. *"I hope that was okay,"* she thought.

"That was wonderful, Lexa, my daughter." Moragah engulfed her in warm loving energy like a mother's hug. Lexa sighed with contentment and relaxed. "So, do you have a plan for today, my priestess?"

"Today, Lady, I plan to make a plan. You've given me life and powers that only happen in books. I need to learn what they are and how to use them. I also need to keep a sharp eye out. That man will come for me again; I know he will. That's why I came home, so he'd come for me in a place where I feel familiar. Darn it, I wish I was rich and had a fancy surveillance system."

"Do you need such a thing?"

"It wouldn't hurt." Lexa felt Moragah's mirth and she, too, smiled. "Okay, what have I missed?"

"What would your favorite heroine do?"

"Easy. She'd meditate and see everything around her with her eyes closed. Wait, are you saying I can do that, too?" For an answer, Moragah just gave her another wave of warm loving energy then withdrew to let her work. "Great," Lexa sighed aloud. "She gave me a fancy bicycle, but no training wheels. Okay, let's give it a try."

She sank to a cross-legged position on the floor and closed her eyes. She took a few deep breaths, then tried to picture the hallway outside her door. The image flickered for a second, then cleared. Amazed, Lexa watched as another resident emerged and locked her door before walking to the elevator. The elevator went up instead of down.

Next she tried the stairs, although she rarely used them. She saw a young couple, teenagers, in the stairwell, kissing. She moved her awareness on to the parking garage. It was empty of people, but there was a note on the windshield of her old car. "Miss Condon, you rent is two weeks past due." Oh crap. "Wait, I could read that. There's the proof I need." Lexa leaped to her feet and ran from the apartment. She fairly danced down the stairs. "Hey, break it up, you two," she said, as she passed the kissing teens. The boy told her to fuck off. Ignoring him, she ran on. The note was on her car, just as she'd seen. "Oh my god, it's real."

"Of course it is," came Moragah's amused voice.

Lexa laughed and danced around. "Oh man, this is so cool. Moragah, you rock." She took the elevator back to her floor. The door had locked behind her. "Oh crap. Now I have to go ask Mr. Jones to open the door and I don't have the rent. Dammit. Wait, maybe I don't." Lexa focused her mind on the door, picturing the locks turning from the other side of the door. She heard the click as it unlocked. Another victory dance followed as she swung the door open wide.

Lexa stopped dancing and sank gracefully to the floor again. "Now for the rent." All her attempts to magic up the rent failed, and she finally gave up. "Okay, that one's a bust. How am I going to get the darn rent? I could go out at night and unlock the doors to the bank? No, I'm not supposed to be a burglar, I'm supposed to be a super hero. Maybe I could save somebody, and they could reward me..., no, that would be wrong too, I guess. What then? Maybe I should ask the boss. Moragah?"

"I am here, Lexa." Moragah's voice clearly conveyed her amusement.

"You're having way too much fun at my expense."

"I'm truly enjoying you, Lexa. I'm quite proud of you. You're doing fine."

"Fine? I'm about to become homeless."

"As was Penny in the early days, and Tasha as well."

"How did they survive? I mean, what did they do for money?"

"They took it from the villains they defeated. They still do."

"Okay, so if I dress up a bit then go out to the bad part of town I could... No, that would be wrong. It would make me like them. I have to find somebody to rescue then I can take the money from the bully, right?"

"You could do that."

"I get the impression you wouldn't approve. Me neither, really. Dang it..." At that point Lexa heard a noise at her door. She couldn't see it from where she sat, but her extra sight kicked in. It was the assassin breaking in. Lexa's eyes grew wide with terror, but she caught herself. "No, I can take this guy and he has information I need." By this time he was inside, closing the door softly behind him.

He saw her as she rose from the floor. He raised his gun, but she thrust a hand towards him and spoke a single word in a deep, demonic voice. "Dragon!" He screamed in terror as the dark serpentine beast rose above him, great jaws opening wide, head thrusting forward as the foot-long fangs reached for his body. He emptied his gun into the ceiling then fell to the floor as the jaws of death closed on him. He did not move again.

Lexa swallowed hard and approached him carefully. She'd seen the dragon, but only as an illusion. To the assassin it had been real. He had literally died of fright. Lexa checked for a pulse and found none. "Shit." She stomped her foot in frustration. "I needed information, not a body. Now what the hell am I going to do? Think, Lexa, think. Okay, check his pockets."

She emptied his pockets then took stock. There were two extra magazines for the gun, fully loaded, the gun with silencer, but she had no idea how to use it. Ah well. There was a wad of cash totaling eight hundred dollars; that, she could use. Chewing gum, lighter - but no smokes, car key - a rental, and a hotel key. "Hmm, might learn something there."

Lexa grabbed the phone book and looked up the hotel's location. She nodded then grabbed her coat. She swung by the manager's suite to pay the rent with the cash she'd taken from the body, then headed for her car. She stepped into the parking area and froze. "What if he put a bomb under my car? Shit, now what am I going to do? Wait, his car. He wouldn't have put a bomb in that, and I might get some information from it. Okay, where is it?"

Heading for the guest parking spaces she held the keys up and pressed the button. There was a soft toot of a horn and a car's lights flickered. "Nice ride," she said, as she settled herself inside. She pulled out onto the street, then drove to the hotel. She parked the car then began to search it. The search turned up nothing, so she headed inside and went up to the room.

The room contained a few of the man's personal belongings. Clothes with no labels, a watch and wedding ring in the pocket of a suit jacket. Further patting down of the jacket turned up a small cell phone. It had a message on it. "Is it done?"

"No, it bloody well isn't," she muttered, as she searched the rest of his clothes. Nothing further turned up, except the soft breathing of a human being. The sounds of those careful breaths slowly penetrated Lexa's awareness. She stepped into the bathroom and closed her eyes. There it was, a woman with a gun, hiding behind the floor length drapes. "Come out from behind those drapes if you want to survive. Toss the gun first."

For a moment nothing happened, then the gun thumped onto the floor and the woman stepped out where she could be seen. Lexa came out of the bathroom holding the empty gun with the silencer on it. "Step away from the gun and sit on the bed. Good girl, now, who are you and what are you doing here?"

"I could ask you the same question."

"Fair enough, you first."

The woman gave her a puzzled look then shrugged. "My name is Ellen Cameron. I'm a private detective. I've been hired by your boyfriend's wife to catch him in the act."

"The act of what?"

"Adultery."

"Oh. Okay, got any ID?" Slowly, carefully the woman pulled her ID out of her jacket pocket and tossed it onto the other bed near Lexa. Lexa flipped it open and inspected it for a moment then tossed the empty gun on the bed beside it. "Okay, my turn, I guess. A few days ago this guy shot and killed my neighbors. I heard something and went to look. He shot me too, but didn't finish me. He tried twice more since that, but failed both times. That's his gun, I took it off his dead body."

"Really?"

"Really."

"You must be a lot tougher than you look, kid."

"Apparently, I am. My name's Lexa Condon and I really need your help."

"My help?" Lexa nodded. "Okay, how can I help? I don't come cheap, you know. I have expenses and..."

"Wait. Hush, someone's coming." Footsteps approached the door and stopped. Lexa waved her hand, indicating the woman should step back. They heard the key in the lock and Lexa waved her hand.

The man who should have been there suddenly appeared with a naked woman in his arms. The door swept open, two shots were fired from a gun with silencer and the couple fell. The gun withdrew and the door closed tightly. Lexa let the vision of the two people fade as she sighed and sat heavily on the bed.

"Sweet Christ," breathed the detective. "How the hell did you do that? Who are you? What are you?"

"I already told you; my name's Lexa and I'm scared to death. Can we get out of here and talk some place safe. I'll tell you everything and explain how we can help each other."

The detective scooped up her gun. "Good idea, let's go." Lexa started to follow her to the door. "That got your finger prints on it?" She was pointing to the gun with silencer on the bed. Lexa nodded. "Better bring it for now. Keep it out of sight."

They rode down the elevator then walked out to the parking lot. "You got a car?"

"Just the guy's rental," replied Lexa. "It's over there. I took it because I was afraid he might have put a bomb in mine."

"Okay. Leave it for now, but we'll have to get your prints out of there too. For now we'll take mine." She led Lexa to a small but fast looking car and they got inside. Ellen started the engine and pulled out into traffic. She went to a drive through and bought coffee for them both then parked the car. "All right, I'm listening," she said, as she passed one coffee to Lexa.

New Job

L exa closed her eyes and called. "Moragah?"

"I am here, Lexa."

"Moragah, I need this woman's help, but I'm not sure if I can trust her."

"You are wise to be cautious, my priestess, but you are correct. You need this woman's help. Yes, she can be trusted. Learn well what she can teach." With that Moragah pulled back and Lexa opened her eyes. Once she started to speak, her story came spilling out of her.

"CIA spooks? Something fishy? You're the witness need to be eliminated? A goddess? Girl, I'll give you points for imagination. The bit about the dragon was good though. I liked that part."

"You don't believe me."

"Not a word. A goddess?"

At Moragah's urging Lexa reached over and grasped Ellen's hand. Suddenly Ellen felt the vast presence of Moragah engulf her, filling her with loving feelings, like a child held by its mother. "I am Moragah, goddess of wisdom, defender of the weak. You are Ellen Cameron who was Elmira Cameron until eight years ago when you changed the name you hated. You have a defective valve in your heart and expect it to claim your life at any time. Release your fear. I have repaired that for you."

"Thank you, Lady Goddess," murmured Ellen, as she sighed dreamily.

"And now you can repay me, Ellen, by listening to Lexa with an open mind." With that Moragah withdrew and Lexa released the woman's hand.

Ellen blinked her eyes and shook off the euphoria. "Wow. I'll give you this, girl, you sure are a master of illusion."

"Yes I am, but Moragah's no illusion. She's real and I can prove it. Call your doctor."

"What???"

"Call your doctor. Tell him you felt a flutter in your chest and you want him to check out the damaged valve."

"Shit, you're not bluffing, are you?"

"Nope. For my illusions to work I have to be in the room with you, like at the hotel room. Here's my phone number, call me when you get the results. Right now I have to go home and do something with the body in my living room."

"Aw, hell. This will probably get me killed, but... we have to get rid of that body. Which way?" She started the car and Lexa pointed the way. They arrived to find three police cars there and the coroner's van.

"I'd say they found the body. Quick, call the police and report the break in."

"What? Are you serious?"

"Yes. Tell them the truth. It'll get a bit weird, but if he died of fright, no marks on him, they've got no reason to hold you."

"Okay, but they'll be pissed I took his gun and car then went to the hotel."

"Oh yes, they will. They'll make a fuss about tampering with evidence, but they've got no real reason to play hardball with you."

"What are you going to do?" asked Lexa, as she got out of the car.

"Make a doctor's appointment. Oh, when you talk to the cops, I'd appreciate it if you didn't mention my name. I wouldn't say anything about a dragon or goddess either." As she drove away, Ellen wondered what she'd gotten herself into. "Dammit, why do I always fall for the weird straight chicks? She sure is cute, though."

Two days later, Lexa was released with a warning not to leave town. She was facing charges of tampering with evidence, but they let her go. Her innocence was gone as well. She had faced long and harsh questioning, had been accused of everything, including murder and conspiracy to commit murder. Suddenly it had stopped. Cold.

There was a soft tap on the door of the interrogation room, a few quiet words were exchanged, then the cop turned back to her. "You're free to go. Don't leave town." He walked away, leaving the door open.

The police hadn't learned anything new from her, but Lexa had learned a lot. She'd learned she was strong. She'd withstood the intimidation tactics as well as the good cop/bad cop routine, and seen through it all. They'd kept her tired, hungry, and thirsty, but it gained them nothing. She'd been on the edge of calling the dragon and walking away when it all stopped.

Lexa could guess why they had let her go. Someone higher up had ordered it. She would be followed and killed. Not going to happen. She walked down the steps of the police station and into the throng of people on the street. She was watched as she stepped out into traffic and hailed a cab. On the sidewalk an old woman smiled as a car pulled out and followed the cab away. She grinned to herself as she got on the bus.

If anyone followed the bus they would never see the old woman again. It was a teenager who bounced off the bus and headed down the street, gazing at her phone the whole time. The girl vanished in the crowd. A moment later Lexa was relaxing in the chair as a hairdresser buzzed off her hair to match the short hair covering her scar. The police and the bad guys were used to seeing her with a kerchief on her head.

The next morning, Ellen Cameron arrived at her office to find Lexa asleep on the couch. "How the hell did you get in here?"

"Through the door. Is the coffee ready yet?"

"Oh, for Christ's sake." Ellen continued to mutter as she made a pot of coffee then returned to the reception area. "There, the coffee's on. Now, how did you find me? How did you get in here?"

Lexa sat up and stiffened her back. "Why don't we talk about why you abandoned me to the wolves first. Christ, they held me for two days, accused me of everything under the sun, including murder, before they let me go."

"Did they actually physically hurt you?"

"What? Well, no, but..."

"But nothing. Girl, you're way too soft to survive what you've gotten yourself into. Facing a real grilling by the cops would either break you or toughen you up." Suddenly Ellen grinned. "Looks like you survived it, all right. Did you tell them about the dragon?"

Lexa had to laugh. "No, but I did catch the odd nap while they badgered an illusion of me. God only knows what the surveillance tapes show."

"Ah, coffee's ready. How do you take it?"

"Sweet and creamy." Ellen passed her a mug and Lexa inhaled with obvious delight. "Okay, how I found you. Cameron's Detective Agency? Really wasn't that hard to find."

"Okay, but I did lock the place up."

"Yeah, well, all I have to do is think hard at a lock and Bam! It's open. I locked up again after I came in. Nobody followed me here, Ellen. I swear it. I changed my appearance several times on the way. So, how's the heart valve?"

"Good as new and nobody knows why. All right, Lexa, as crazy as it sounds, I do believe your story. Your goddess is real, and I feel better than I have in years. You said you wanted my help. Girl, somehow you stumbled on some very high-level government spooks cleaning house. You're a loose end, a wild card and that makes them nervous. I don't want to get caught up in that."

"No, I don't want you to either," replied Lexa. She took another long appreciative sip from her mug then went on. "Ellen, Moragah made me what I am so I could go after the bad guys at the top. The problem is, I have no idea at all how to find them. That's where you come in."

"Okay, how?"

"Take me on as your assistant, teach me how to investigate, gather information, locate people. Once you think I'm ready, then I can step out on my own and go after the guys I need to find."

"Lexa, the guys at the top are the government, never doubt that. That or they control the government. Oh, what the hell. All right, here's the deal. You work for me. I'll pay you standard rate, plus you can stay at my place. I have lots of room. You won't dare go back to your apartment."

"Yeah, I know. Ellen, can I have a small advance? I need some clothes and... well, you know."

Ellen sat back and looked at her for a long moment then sighed. "All right, Mother Goddess, or whatever your name is, I'll do this. I need to restore the balance, at least." She rose and extended her hand to Lexa. "Come on, Mistress of Shadows, let's go."

"Sure. Where are we going?"

"Shopping. You need clothes, and maybe even a new name."

"New name? Why?"

"Because Lexa Condon needs to disappear. Come on." They met the receptionist on their way out. "Debbie, I'll be out of the office all day. Juggle whatever you need to and fake the rest. We'll be back tomorrow." The girl was still staring open mouthed as Ellen took Lexa's elbow and hustled her towards the car.

"What is your mother's maiden name?"

"Elmore, why?"

"Okay, what's your middle name?"

"Seline."

"Pretty, I like it. From now on, you're Seline Elmore. Got it?"

"Okay, sure. I like it, but what about my ID and stuff."

"Let me worry about that for now. Ah, here we are. Little red sports car."

The newly named Seline Elmore settled into the passenger's seat, admiring the car. "Wow, some ride. What happened to the one you had the other day?"

"Old Betsy? I only drive Betsy when I'm trying to go unnoticed. Today we're going shopping."

It was late in the day when they arrived at Ellen's high-rise condo. Seline flopped onto the expensive looking sofa, her many packages spilling around her, and gazed in wonder at the view, both inside and out. "Like it?" asked Ellen.

"Oh my god, I've dreamed of living in a place like this. Ellen, I don't know what to say."

"Come on, I have one more thing to show you then I'll let you rest. We've got your new ID and that'll stand up to most scrutiny, your new driver's license, a P.I. badge, new clothes, and tomorrow we begin to build the new identity. Your public identity."

"Public identity? You mean I'm going to have a private one?"

"A secret one."

"Like Batman."

"Yes, indeed. Here we are, what do you think?"

Seline was stunned. She was in the library, and it was over flowing. She began to look at some of the titles and recognized a few old favorites. "Ellen?"

"Yes, I'm a fantasy adventure junkie, just like you. You like it?"

"Like it? Woman, I'm in heaven."

Ellen chuckled with delight. "Come on, Seline. Let's raid the kitchen. I'll tell you what I have in mind while we eat."

"Deal," replied Seline, enjoying the sound of her new name. She tried to puzzle it all out while she watched Ellen prepare a quick meal and serve it up.

"What's wrong, Seline? You look confused, even a bit frightened. What is it?"

"It's you. Don't get me wrong here; I'm loving the new clothes, the new name, and this place is pure magic."

"But?"

"This morning it was like someone threw a switch. Before that you were reserved, wary, and perhaps a bit frightened of me. What happened there?"

"I gave myself a swift kick in the pants," replied Ellen. She sat to the table and smiled at Seline. "Look, I realized you saved my life at that hotel, and I thanked you by throwing you to the sharks, as you put it. Girl, you actually introduced me to a real goddess, and she fixed me. Perhaps you don't know what that valve thing meant. It was like a bomb that could go off at any second. Every moment of my life, every breath, was borrowed time. And then She fixed me.

"You saved my life, and then She gave me new life. I believe in balance, and I can't begin to tell you just how far out of balance this thing with us really is. Today was my first step in trying to restore that balance. I'll give you a new identity, a secret identity, a home, and I'll teach you what I can. A life for a life, Lady Shadow, that's what I'm offering you. Shall we face the adventure together?"

Seline was awestruck. This beautiful, successful woman had just made her an offer she couldn't refuse. "You sound like one of the heroes from my books."

The voice of Moragah whispered in Seline's mind. "Accept her, my priestess. You need her. There is more to this woman than I first realized. I am well pleased with her."

A wave of relief swept over Seline. "Moragah says it's a deal. Ellen, I don't know what to say here. I..."

"Relax, girl. I inherited a ton of money. I became a private detective because I wanted a bit of excitement before the leaky valve took me out. With that fixed, I can relax and enjoy the ride. From what I can gather of your mission in life, it should be exciting to say the least."

"You mean pretty short and scary as hell. So tell me, what did you mean about a secret identity?"

"Lexa Condon is gone, never to be seen again. Your goddess changed her into you, Seline Elmore, but only you and I know that. You're my new protege from out west, here to learn the trade from me. You live with me here. You're a private detective, nothing more.

"However, there is something else loose in the city now, tracking silent assassins, dealing judgment upon the powers behind the dealers of death. She's Lady Shadow, master of illusion and so much more."

Seline giggled then sighed. "Keep talking. I'll never have to read a book again."

Ellen laughed as she rose to gather the dishes and put them in the machine. "Okay, you got me; I'm a closet fantasy writer. I admit that was a bit over the top, but you get the idea."

Seline turned to smile at her. "Yes, I think I do. Just give me a minute." She focused for a moment then something moved in the shadows. Startled, Ellen turned and backed away. The figure of a woman stepped into the light. She was tall with up-swept ears and long graceful fingers. Long flowing robes of scarlet clothed her body, the hood hiding one side of her features.

Slowly, she pushed back the hood to expose long red hair caught back in a thick braid and eyes of icy green. She smiled, exposing long canine teeth, but the smile didn't reach her eyes. She exuded an aura of danger, of impending death. A single word escaped her perfect lips. "Areoth!"

At that word the shadows beside her coalesced into a large serpentine beast, heavily scaled and with dripping fangs. Eyes of fire blazed menacingly from the creature, and it was clear that only the woman's hand on its back held the beast in check. "I'm called Lady Shadow. Speak only truth, for Aeroth will know if you lie. He doesn't like it."

Suddenly, Seline noticed the look of terror on Ellen's face. She quickly dismissed the illusion and leaped to her friend's side, gently guiding her into a chair. "Breathe, girl, breathe."

Ellen swallowed hard, then spoke. Her voice came out a high pitched squeak. "Oh my fucking god."

"Wine. You need wine. Where...?" Ellen pointed and Seline found a bottle. A quick search turned up the opener. A moment later, she placed a glass in Ellen's hand. It took both hands to steady the glass on its way to her lips, but Ellen managed it. She took a long sip, swallowed, took a deep breath, then drained the glass, carefully placing the empty glass back on the table. Grinning, Seline refilled it then sat facing the distraught woman. "Was that something like what you meant?"

Ellen's voice had fully returned. "Oh yeah, that'll do just fine."

"Sorry I scared you."

"The hell you are. You're laughing at me. Jesus, Seline, I had no real idea. Wow. What else can you do?"

"Well, I'm super strong." She lifted the heavy dining table with ease to demonstrate. "I can hear stuff from quite a distance by concentrating, and I can move so fast you can't see me do it. Oh, and I can close my eyes and see everything around me. That's how I knew that guy was going to come into the hotel room shooting. I could see him pull a mask over his face and put the silencer on his gun. Moragah says there is more stuff, but I have to figure it out on my own."

"Wow. Okay. What the hell did you need me for if you can do all that?"

"Up until a few days ago, I was just an unemployed waitress; a burger flipper looking for a job, no family, no friends, and no prospects. My idea of heaven was to find a library and hide out there forever, living my life between the pages. I have no real life experience, and I've no idea at all what the hell I'm doing.

"Ellen, I'm so lost here. I'm a five-year-old with the keys to the gun cabinet. A lot of innocent people could get hurt while I try to figure things out on my own. I need a mentor, a guide, someone to trust, someone I can talk to who knows about me. Someone to keep me grounded. I need you more than you know. Please help me."

"Okay, but you've got to stop scaring the crap out of me. I see now what happened to that guy in your apartment. Help me finish this bottle of wine, then we'll call it a day. Tomorrow, Seline Elmore starts her new job as a detective."

First Case

Seline awakened abruptly as the drapes in her room were thrust aside to let in the dazzling sunlight. "What the... oh god, you're a morning person, aren't you?"

Ellen beamed her a dazzling smile. "Coffee's on. Day's a-wasting. Rise and shine."

Seline groaned then suddenly jumped out of bed and stepped to the window. "I almost forgot." She faced the sun, spread her arms wide and began a morning prayer. "Great Lady Moragah, thank you for this wonderful new home, a good night's sleep, and the coffee waiting for me downstairs. Thank you especially for Ellen and her generosity. May your name be forever blessed." She lowered her arms and turned back to the room. "Hope that was okay."

"It was wonderful, my priestess. So, you are Seline now. So be it." With a wave of loving energy for Seline, Moragah withdrew.

Noticing Ellen watching her closely, Seline shrugged. "Sorry. I need to do that every day. Moragah gives a lot but doesn't ask a lot in return. Just a morning prayer."

Ellen nodded thoughtfully. "Then She shall have it from both of us from now on. Get dressed, girl, coffee's waiting."

"Okay, what does the well-dressed private detective wear, from all this you bought me yesterday?" Ellen threw open the closet, tossed out underwear, pantyhose, a simple but elegant suit in navy blue. The shoes and simple silver jewelry followed. Seline dressed, ran a brush across her short buzz cut, then followed Ellen down to the kitchen for breakfast.

It proved to be an exciting day for Seline. She was introduced to the other investigators and the receptionist, sat in during report, joined a meeting with a client, and was given her first case.

As they were returning from lunch, a middle aged woman, plainly dressed, stood up as they entered. "This is Mrs. Clayton," said Debbie, the receptionist. "She doesn't have an appointment, but your two o'clock is late. Could you possibly fit her in?"

The woman looked on hopefully. She stepped closer. "Please, you have to help me."

With a reassuring smile, Ellen indicated the door to her inner office. "Right this way, ma'am." They stepped inside and Seline closed the door behind them. "Please be seated," said Ellen, as she took her place behind the desk. Seline sat to the side, watching carefully.

Ellen leaned her arms on the desk. When she spoke, her voice was warm and comforting. "Tell me, how can we be of service?"

"It's my daughter," Mrs. Clayton began, "she's disappeared. No one knows where she is. I'm terrified something has happened to her."

"Have you been to the police?" asked Ellen. "Filed a missing person report?"

"Oh no, I wouldn't dare involve the police."

"Tell me all of it." Some of the warmth had left Ellen's voice.

The woman pushed a picture of a pretty girl's high school graduation across the desk. "This is Monica. That was taken last year. She was such a happy girl. She went off to college last fall. Everything seemed fine until spring break. She came home and I could tell something was wrong. I tried to tell my husband, but he wouldn't listen. They fought. The next morning she was gone. She took the bus back to the university, but disappeared from there. They contacted us to see if we knew her whereabouts."

"Okay, so why can't you go to the police?"

"My husband would be angry if I did. He's forbidden it. Harold is a very devout man, a pillar of the church, and a stern man. He and Monica had words. Monica ran to her room, crying, and the next morning she was gone.

"I have some money I've saved from the household expenses over the years. I can pay you. Please help me."

She was reaching into her purse as Ellen spoke. "Our fees are five hundred dollars per day, plus expenses."

The woman's face fell. "Oh. Oh dear. Do you think you could find her in one day? That's all I have."

Once again, Ellen gave that reassuring smile. "This woman is Seline Elmore, my assistant. Seline has just acquired her investigator's license. She needs the practice, so it will be her case with me supervising. We'll give you two days for the price of one. That will double our chances of success. Does that work for you?"

"Oh my goodness, yes. Thank you so much." She turned to Seline. "Do you think you can find her?"

"I can't promise, but I'll do my level best," replied Seline. "Tell me about her. What were her hobbies, did she work when in high school? What sorts of jobs did she do?" Ellen sat back and smiled with delight as Seline gently probed for more information. The girl had good instincts.

"Well, do you want to start at the university?" Ellen asked, as soon as they were alone in the office.

Seline thought for a moment before responding. "No," she replied. She sighed and sat back in her chair. "If I'm wrong about this I'll waste an afternoon. If I'm right I'll find her in a couple of hours."

"Oh really, Miss Super Sleuth. Care to share your reasoning?"

"Don't play coy with me; I know you read this one like I did. Girl grows up in a strict household, goes off to Uni and discovers the sweet taste of freedom. She goes to a party, gets drugged, raped, and goes home where she should find a safe haven. Dad starts thumping the bible, she realizes she can't tell anyone what happened, but starts to blubber anyway. They brand her a slut or worse. God help her if she's pregnant and wants an abortion. She runs back to the city.

"She can't go back to school; she can't face the people who did that to her. She heads for a women's shelter and they help her get the abortion, then find her a job. All she has experience doing is flipping burgers so I'll probably find her pouring coffee at the closest greasy spoon to the shelter."

Ellen grinned with delight. "Girl, you've got good instincts. Did I detect a bit of past experience there?"

"Yeah, that could be my life story all right. Close enough, anyway. However, here's my problem. Why do they really want to find her?"

"What do you mean?" Ellen's smile was even wider. Oh yeah, Seline had good instincts all right.

"They didn't alert the police. Why not? If they truly wanted to find her they'd have gone to the police first, then come to us if that failed. No, she came here alone. I see two possibilities here. First, she wants to find her daughter and is afraid to tell her husband. I doubt that one."

"Why?"

"If the man is as controlling as she claims, how did she manage to hide that much money from him? No, I believe he sent her here himself."

"Why would he do that?" Ellen was still grinning with pride at her protege.

"My best guess?" replied Seline. "I'd say they're part of a strict church, a real cult. They probably want to find her so they can capture her, take her somewhere, pray the demons out of her, and make her somebody's obedient little bride. Probably one of the older men has an eye on her and is willing to take her even though she's tainted."

Ellen gazed at her for a moment. "Forgive me, Seline, but that sounds like more experience talking."

"Close, but I got away. That was three years ago. So, tell me I'm wrong."

"Oh, you're not wrong. That's the way I read it, too. However, that leaves us with a dilemma."

"Which is?"

"Do we find her? If we do, we have to report it to the mother. We can't hold out or hold back on a client."

Seline sighed deeply and studied her hands for a moment. "So, do we find her, get paid, then go on to the next case? I guess that's how this job works, right? We can't get involved; it's none of our business once the job is done, right?"

"Sadly, that is correct. However, sometimes it's really hard to do. This is your case, what do you want to do?"

"My first instinct is to make a show of searching, but make sure I don't find her. I know, I know, that's unethical and I can't do it. I could just turn her in and walk away, job done."

"But you can't do that either, can you?"

"Not and live with myself."

"So, where does that leave you?"

"Ellen, if I wasn't here what would have done?"

"Told her I couldn't help until after the police had given up."

"But you took the case to test me."

"Yes, I did. Seline, you wanted my help. Your mission in life will take you up against some dangerous people. You need to hone your skills in actual field operations."

"So the Lady of Shadows and her pet dragon need to get involved?"

"Admit it, that was your plan anyway."

Seline laughed. "Okay, it was. I'll go see if I can find her then head these fools off, make sure they leave her alone."

"Take the older car, it's outside at the end of the parking lot. Debbie has the keys at her desk. I'll tell her to give you some cash from the slush fund as well. You'll need it. Remember to keep all receipts."

"Yes, ma'am." Seline saluted then stepped out to reception. She heard as Ellen gave Debbie instructions. She collected the cash and keys then left the building.

Seline knew the location of the women's shelter near the university. She drove by but didn't stop. They would tell her nothing; it was pointless to ask. Seline parked and sat thinking for a minute. "I wonder, could it be that easy?" Hell, it was worth a shot. She'd originally gotten the job at Dick's Cafe from the shelter. Maybe this girl had taken her old job. She pulled back into traffic, then drove the two blocks to the small cafe where she'd spent three years trying to keep the owner's hands off her ass.

Seline altered her appearance slightly, then got out of the car. As she entered the cafe, a large man glanced up then spoke. "What the hell are you doing back here?"

Seline fought to keep the grin off her face as she responded. "Excuse me?"

Looking closely at her, he suddenly began to backpedal. "Oh shit, sorry, ma'am, I thought you were somebody else."

"Obviously. Now that you're paying attention, I'm a private detective. I'm looking for this girl; have you seen her?"

"What? Oh yeah, that's Trudy. She's back in the kitchen. I'll just get her for you."

As he turned away, Seline moved at super speed. A moment later a young woman ran towards the back door, but Seline was blocking her path. "Nice try, sister." She grinned as she took the frightened girl by the arm. "I'm not here to hurt you, I just want to talk." She ushered the girl to a booth and settled her in. The cafe owner approached, but Seline handed him fifty dollars and pointed at the kitchen. He got the message.

Seline slid into the booth facing the frightened girl. "I'm Seline Elmore, private detective. You, on the other hand, are Monica

Clayton." The girl swallowed hard and nodded. "Your mother hired me to find you. Job done. I can see that you're scared. Tell me why."

"Please, don't tell them where I am."

"Sorry, I have to. That's how I get paid. However, there's more going on here than a simple runaway. You're scared, way too scared for things to be all that simple. Tell me what's going on, maybe I can help."

"Why would you?"

"I couldn't tell you, cause I don't really know for sure. It's just that this case stinks, it has from the start. Tell me what's going on."

The girl sighed deeply then gave in, her posture sagging, her eyes fixed on her hands as she spoke. "It's an old story, really. Young, naive, girl, raised in a strict religious family, goes off to college, gets drunk, gets raped, runs home."

"But there's no shelter there?"

"No, I'm a slut, a whore, unworthy. The deacon will marry me and make me an honest woman, but first the demons have to be exorcised from my body. Look, I didn't do anything wrong, except trust the wrong people. They hurt me and now I'm facing a life I'd rather die than face. If they find me I'm done for. They'll come for me and..."

"Okay, I get it." Seline looked thoughtful for a moment. "Look, the world's a much bigger and scarier place than either you or I realize. There's someone who owes me a favor. If you'll trust me, I'll contact this person before I report that I found you. You stick to your routine and let my contact do the rest. I promise you; they won't get you, and they'll never try a second time. After that you're on your own. Your life will be whatever you make of it."

"You mean it? You'll really help me? How can I trust that?"

"Look, girl, you don't have a lot of options here. Consider this, if I wasn't telling the truth, why would I even talk to you? All I had to do was see your face, buy a coffee, walk out that door and make my report. That easy. Someone gave me a chance once, now I'm offering you one. Take it or leave it, it's up to you."

"All right, I'll trust you. If this is real, I can live my life without looking over my shoulder every minute of every day. If not, I'll find a way to end this life, but I will not be sold to that creepy old man."

"Fair enough," smiled Seline. "Go through the rest of your day as per normal. I'll be watching. Tomorrow morning I'll report I've found you and where. There will be someone else watching when you come to work. You'll have a shadow until this is over."

Seline rose, dropped a fifty on the table and walked out. Monica watched as she got in the old car and drove away. When her shift was over, she noticed the same old car follow her back to her apartment.

"Have any luck?" asked Ellen, as Seline let herself back into the condo.

Seline tossed the keys to the old car into the bowl on the hall table, kicked off her shoes, and made her way to the kitchen where she found Ellen busy at the stove. "Yeah, it was too easy, really."

"How so?"

"Like you guessed, her story was a lot like mine. I drove to the shelter near the university then started checking the burger joints nearby. She actually has my old job. She tried to run, but I caught her and we talked. Eventually she agreed to stay put and let me handle the bad guys when they come for her. I said I'd report to her mother first thing tomorrow, then my contact would go on guard duty until it was over."

"Bet she's already on a bus to another city." Ellen grinned as she set a plate of food on the table for Seline."

"Doesn't matter." Seline moaned with delight as she tasted the food. "I have her address and her place of employment. I found her, that's what I get paid to do. I did the job, and I expect to be paid. Besides, they'll never know if she ran or not. Once we make that report I'm vanishing, and Lady Shadow will head downtown and take over. I promise you; they'll never get near her."

"If she runs, how will...?"

"Oh they'll see her, one way or the other. That's why I talked to her for so long, to get her clear in my mind. I also followed her home. I need to be there early so, if she's run, I can change my appearance and take her place."

"Want me to go with you?"

"No, just drop me off in the area then make the report to her mother. I'll deal with the rest then give you a full report when I get home."

Ellen smiled warmly at her friend. "Keeping me out of the action?"

"Nope, making sure no one can make a connection between you and Lady Shadow."

"Can't I watch?"

"Afraid you'll miss some of the excitement?"

"Well, you'll want a ride home when it's over."

"Okay, fair enough, but be safe, okay?"

"You'll never know I'm there." Ellen was grinning with delight. She really did want to watch Lady Shadow in action.

The next morning the old car stopped and a woman got out, thanked the driver for the ride, then faded into the throngs on the street. She was dressed like a student, but she subtly changed several times before she arrived at Monica's apartment where the roommate informed her Monica had left town. Seline nodded, thanked the girl, then turned away. Halfway down the block she changed again. By the time she reached the old cafe she was Monica.

As the day wore on Seline was reminded of how much she'd hated that job. About midway through the shift the boss patted her ass again and she hit him hard in the balls. He dropped to the kitchen floor making sounds like a dog's squeaky toy and folded up in the fetal position. The cook watched with a look of horror on her face. "Next time you grab my ass, I'll tear off your arm and beat you with the wet end. Understand?" The man on the floor squeaked again. She went back to work as though nothing had happened.

At the end of the shift, Seline pocketed her tips then headed back towards Monica's apartment. She was about halfway there when a van pulled up beside her and hands reached out. She easily avoided the grasping hands and fled into an empty parking lot then stopped, facing her pursuers. The van screeched to a halt and five men poured out. "Monica, you must come with us now. Your immortal soul is in peril."

In the shelter of the old building across the street, a woman in a darkened car grinned with delight. As the men advanced on the girl something stirred in the shadows. It took a moment for them to realize someone was standing beside the girl. When they shifted their focus the girl vanished, leaving the tall woman in the flowing crimson robes alone with the five men.

"Who are you?" demanded one of the men.

"They call me Lady Shadow," replied the apparition, as she slowly pushed the hood back from her face, exposing her up swept ears. Her smile didn't reach her eyes, but it did expose her fangs. She gestured with her hand and something else moved in the shadows. The men suddenly clustered closer together as the huge serpentine creature moved into view. "This is Aeroth. I think he's hungry." At that the dragon threw back its head and roared. A huge gout of flame spewed into the night air from its gaping maw.

The men fell back in terror, but the woman stepped towards them. "I've claimed the girl for myself. Pursue her further and Aeroth will have you."

"Begone, Demon from Hell," bellowed one man as he thrust a cross toward her.

She leaped at them then, snatching away the cross and driving it through the door panel of the van. She grabbed the man closest to her and threw him into the parking lot at the dragon's feet. He leaped to his feet and trembling, thrust a bible at the scaled beast. The dragon snorted and the book, as well as the man's coat sleeve, burst into flames. He screamed and backed away, beating at the flames until they were out. The dragon speared the book with a claw, raised it towards his mouth, then snorted fire on it. The book crumbled into ash.

The woman called out and fire began to rain down from the sky. The men fled into the van to sounds of her demonic laughter. The van raced away, and the woman lowered her arms. The fire died. The dragon came to her and rubbed hits great head against her hip. She patted it fondly then it stepped back into the shadows and vanished from sight. Slowly the woman faded into the shadows as well, leaving a tired Seline standing alone in the parking lot.

The old car pulled up and Seline got in, grateful for the ride. "Gods, my feet hurt," she complained. "I forgot how much I despised that job. So, what do you think? Did Lady Shadow put the fear into those guys or what?"

Ellen laughed. "Oh yeah, I don't think they'll be looking for that girl any time soon. That bit where the dragon burned the bible, that was real, wasn't it?"

"Yeah, I can make the dragon's fire real."

"When did you figure that out?"

"About five minutes ago."

"Seline, you scare me." Ellen realized she was talking to herself; Seline had curled up and gone to sleep. "So, using the juice takes the good out of you, does it? I'll have to keep an eye on that. Time to take you home and tuck you in for the night, Lady Shadow."

Catching the Scent

N ext morning, as they entered the office, they got a surprise. Without warning a woman leaped at Seline, swing her heavy purse at her head. "Whore! Murderer!"

Ellen shrieked and ducked, but the blow was meant for Seline. It didn't connect. Seline easily batted aside the purse, then swept the woman into the air and unceremoniously dumped her on the couch. She had the woman's hands pinned in one hand and holding her legs still with the other. Seline had also slightly altered her appearance. "Stop this. Stop struggling."

Slowly the woman ceased her struggles and relaxed. Seline released her and helped her to a sitting position. "Why did you attack me?"

"Because I hate you, you home wrecker. You killed my husband, you slut, murderer."

Ellen stepped forward. "Mrs. Alldon, what makes you think Seline killed your husband? He was found across town, dead of a heart attack."

"The police showed me a picture of the whore he'd been seeing. He was found dead in her apartment. That's her. I came here this morning to settle my account when I saw you two walking in here. I recognized her at once."

"Mrs, Alldon, Seline arrived here the day before yesterday from California. I'm quite certain she's never met your husband."

"Forgive me, ma'am," said Seline, "but that's a lot of emotion to spend on a man you believed to be cheating on you."

"Yes, well, Frank wasn't much to look at, but I loved him; he was all I had." She looked closely at Seline. "Forgive me, you do resemble that other woman, but her eyes were brown, and she had long hair. Your nose is different too. I'm sorry."

Seline smiled. "And I'm sorry I beat you up. Let's start over. I'm Seline Elmore, Ellen's new assistant."

"Jenine Alldon."

"Jenine, tell me about your husband," said Seline. Ellen smiled and stepped away. "What did he do for a living?"

"Oh god, I couldn't tell you." The woman sighed deeply and accepted the glass of water Debbie had brought for her. "Something to do with the government. He never talked about it. I asked a few times when we were first married, but he said he wasn't allowed to talk about his work, government secrecy and all that."

"What about the people he worked with? Did you ever socialize with them?"

"No, well, occasionally someone would come by for a beer, but they always retreated to the man cave to talk shop or football or something. John was the only one I saw several times over the years."

"John?"

"John Daniels, Frank's boss. He came by about once a month over the years. He was at the funeral. He said if there ever was anything I wanted to let him know."

"Do you know how to get in touch with Mr. Daniels?"

"Well, yes, but why? Why are you asking me all these questions?"

Seline laughed and shook her head. She leaned back and held up her hands defensively. "I'm so sorry. It's a habit. It's what I do for a living. I just can't seem to mind my own business. I'll just shut up now and get out of your face." She stood and backed away.

The woman rose to her feet and straightened her skirt. "Yes, well, this is all so embarrassing. I've already written the cheque, so I'll just be on my way." She stepped to the door then stopped and turned back. "Young woman, you tossed me around like a rag doll. How did you get so strong? Even Frank couldn't have done that."

"I work out," grinned Seline. "Weight training can work wonders."

"Right." She turned to the door then stopped again. Turning back, she walked over and went nose to nose with Seline. "I don't trust you. You're up to something and I want to know what it is." Both Ellen and Debbie were wide eyed and trying to signal Seline to clam up. It didn't work.

"Okay, you got me, but I can't tell you much and we never had this conversation, okay?"

"You're serious?"

"I am."

"All right. So what aren't you telling me about my husband's death?"

"Ma'am, I don't know a damn thing about your husband's death. It's my sister I'm trying to find."

"Your sister?"

"My twin. Parents killed in a car crash, both of us adopted out as babies to different families. I learned about her last year, and I've been trying to find a job here on the east coast ever since. When I got a chance to work with Ellen, I leaped at it. I could learn from the best and find my sister to boot. When you jumped me, I knew she's in this city somewhere, but secret government people have a way of making other people disappear. If she's gone missing, this man might know where she's gone."

Mrs Alldon paused for a moment. "You do look like her. But if the government has made her disappear, should you be poking around in this?"

"Probably not and that's why we didn't have this conversation." Mrs. Alldon gazed into her eyes for a long moment then pulled a note pad from her purse. She jotted something down, passed it to Seline, then turned and left without another word. Seline gazed at the note then smiled. It had John Daniels name and phone number on it.

Seline glanced up from the note to see Ellen and Debbie staring at her. "What?"

Before Ellen could speak, Debbie stepped closer to Seline. "How do you do that?"

"Do what?"

"Change your appearance like that. Yesterday you had brown eyes, but now they're blue. Yesterday your nose was straight, but now not so much. Your eyebrows are thicker. How do you do that?" Seline glanced past Debbie to see Ellen grinning. She took Debbie by the hand and led her into the inner office.

"Are you sure you want to know the answer to your question?" she asked. Debbie just nodded.

"You'd better sit down for this, Debbie," said Ellen, as she followed them in and closed the door. Looking fearfully from Seline to Ellen and back again, Debbie sat. Seline nodded then spoke.

"You've heard of Batman, Superman, and others like that, right?"

"Sure.

"So, what do they all have in common?"

"They're super heroes."

"What else?"

Debbie thought for a moment. "They all have secret identities. Are you trying to tell me you're a super hero?"

"No, not a super hero, but something else," replied Seline. "Don't be scared, just watch."

Something moved in the corner of the office. A shadow grew, moving to encompass Seline. Seline grew taller, her ears swept up and back as her fingers grew longer. The shadow approaching became a python that crawled up her leg and wound around her body then slithered down her arm and became an ornate staff. "I'm Lady Shadow," said a full rich voice, very different from Seline's. "Aeroth!"

Debbie sucked in her breath to scream as the dragon came from the shadows. She opened her mouth, but no scream came out, just a soft squeak. "Oh fuck!"

The huge beast moved closer to her, sniffed at her, and then presented his head for petting. "You may touch him," smiled the shadow woman. "He likes you." Hesitantly, Debbie reached out to rub the heavy scales behind the creature's ear. It rumbled a purr then turned back to Seline. "Go back to your rest now, my pet." With another rumbling purr, the beast returned to the shadows and vanished.

"There is more, much more," said Shadow Seline, as she tossed the staff onto the floor. It became a snake and crawled away into the shadows. She began to change again. The flowing robes disappeared, becoming chain mail armor. The woman who stood before Debbie now was heavily muscled and wild eyed. The python that had been on the floor suddenly struck at her, changing into a flaming sword. The woman caught it, spun it about expertly then knelt at Debbie's feet.

"I am Seline of Shadows, Great Lady Deborah. Now that you know my secret, you have the power to help or destroy me. My fate is in your hands." Slowly she changed back into Seline. "That woman's husband wasn't my lover, Debbie, he was a killer. He's the one who put this crease in my skull." She parted her short hair, exposing the scar on her head.

Debbie didn't speak for a moment. "Oh fuck." Ellen passed her a glass of water. She took a long sip, then tried her voice again. "Sweet Betsy Ross, that was scary."

Ellen laughed. "It's all right, Debbie, you can say it."

Debbie was still wild eyed, but getting her breath back. "Goddammit, Seline. You couldn't just tell me first, you had to scare the crap out of me? Sweet baby Jesus. What are you laughing at, Ellen. You've seen this before haven't you? And you didn't warn me?"

"I did tell you to sit down."

"Holy crap." She turned her attention back to Seline who had retreated to a chair. "It's all illusion, right?"

"Most of it," replied Seline.

"Most of it?"

"You touched the dragon. Did he feel real?"

"Well, yes, but that could be an illusion ..." She stopped as Ellen's expletive interrupted her.

"Oh shit, Seline!" exclaimed Ellen. "I just had this carpet installed last month."

Debbie looked down where Ellen was pointing. There was a gash in the carpet. "The dragon's claw," she mused softly.

Seline cringed back in her chair. "I'll pay for it. You can take it out of my wages, right?"

"I'll take it out of your hide the next time," replied Ellen, winking at Debbie. "She gets carried away, Debbie. Now, if Seline's done showing off, we all have work to do. This thing this morning is off the books. Seline's got a private case to work and she'll need our help from time to time, but it's all off the books."

"Damn right it is," sighed Debbie, her voice fully back at last. "Sweet mother of mercy. Okay, Lady Shadow, the file name is dragon. Verbal only. Anything you need, any time, just ask."

"Thanks, Debbie. I'm trusting you with my life here."

"Yeah, yeah, sure, sure. Ellen, you told me when we started this agency it would be exciting, but this is way over the top. Imagine, we've got our own super hero on staff." Seline grinned as Debbie regained her natural exuberance and headed back to her desk.

They waited until Debbie had closed the door, then Ellen turned to Seline. "So, you've got your first lead. Girl, we're going to have to be extremely careful here."

"I know." Seline sighed and fairly melted into a chair. "Here's the thing. I have no desire to go after this guy unless he's the one who ordered my execution."

Ellen shook her head. "I don't think there's much doubt of that."

Seline nodded. "Yeah, but, in their minds I'm just a loose end. Why were the Browns killed? That's the question I'd like answered."

"Can you tell me anything about that?"

"I heard them shouting next door. Mr. Brown knew about something and wanted to tell the authorities. The other guy wanted him to shut up and say nothing. I heard a popping sound, a woman screamed, the popping sound again, then silence. Like an idiot, I went next door to see if they needed help. I knocked on the door, got yanked inside and shot. I woke up in a puddle of my own blood."

Ellen pondered for a moment. "So your neighbor wanted to be a whistle blower and paid the price."

"That's about it. What do you think I should do?"

"Well, I'm sure confronting him will gain us nothing. If he is a CIA spook, he'll never talk, not to a couple of P.I.s."

"A couple of P.I.s? Oh no you don't. This one is mine, Ellen. You have to stay miles away from this."

"Okay, okay, relax, Lady Shadow. I was just thinking out loud. Look, I think we'll learn more by following this guy than we will by direct confrontation."

"There's that *we* again."

"Sorry."

"Explain. Why follow him instead of beating it out of him?"

"Because he'll never talk. However, if we shadow him for a while we might find out what he's up to that would alert a whistle blower."

Just then, there was a soft tap on the door, Debbie stepped in and passed Seline a slip of paper, then she returned to her desk, closing the door behind her. Seline smiled as she read the note. "That our man's address?" asked Ellen, a smile playing at her lips.

"Indeed it is."

"Told you Debbie could work magic."

Not That Easy

Seline drove the old car to the address Debbie had given her. It was an empty lot. She vented her frustration with a few choice words then called the office. "It's a bust, Debbie."

"Address a warehouse or an empty lot?"

"Empty lot," replied Seline.

"Dammit. Okay, Ellen's out of the office. You can reach her on the cell."

"Cool. Thanks, Debbie." Seline broke the connection and called Ellen. "Hi, it's me. It's a bust. Empty lot. Are you having any fun?"

"Sitting in my car with a camera in my lap. My guy is in a motel with a gal. I'll get pics as they come out. Could be a while. Go back to the office, Debbie might have something for you."

"On my way. Later."

Seline arrived at the office to find Debbie on the phone. She poured herself a mug of coffee then sat quietly to wait. Debbie was listening, taking notes, and muttering, "got it" in the appropriate places. Seline allowed her attention to wander until she set the phone back on its cradle. A man stepped through the door at that point.

"Good afternoon, sir. How can we be of service?" asked Debbie.

"Is this woman a client of yours?" he asked, showing Debbie a picture.

Debbie's eyes widened and she swallowed hard. "Yes," she replied cautiously. "That's Mrs. Alldon. She was here today."

"I'll need all her files and a full statement of your business with her."

46

Seline had risen and peered past the man's shoulder. The picture was of Mrs. Alldon, dead, her eyes wide open and a bullet hole in her forehead. "Who are you? What do you want here? Our receptionist isn't giving you anything until Ms. Cameron is present and you have a court order."

"I'm Agent John Daniels, FBI. If you try to stall me you'll be charged with obstructing justice."

"Let's see your ID." He pulled out an ID packet and flipped it open for a second then closed it. "Not so fast. Pass that to Debbie so she can check it out."

He began to bluster as Ellen returned. "What's going on?" she asked. He repeated his story then showed her the picture. Ellen nodded. "What happened to her?"

"That's what we're trying to find out. Every moment is crucial. I need those files."

"Of course," Ellen replied. "Debbie, give Agent Daniels everything we have on Mrs. Alldon."

Debbie rose to retrieve the files. "What was your business with Mrs. Alldon?" asked the agent.

"I handled that case personally. She hired me to follow her husband, to find out if he was cheating on her."

"What did you find out?"

"I found him dead in his girlfriend's apartment, surrounded by police."

Seline watched carefully. Debbie was listening to Ellen speak, then her fingers flew over the keyboard. Soon the printer began to spit out a few pages. She put them in a folder then passed it to the agent. "This all of it?"

"Yes, that's all of it."

"Delete the e-files."

"What?"

"Ladies, this is a federal investigation. I have the hard copies. This needs to be kept quiet until the case is closed. Delete the files and stay away from this case." Ellen nodded and Debbie hit the delete key. The agent nodded and walked out.

Seline started to follow, but Ellen stopped her. "Seline, no. Not now, he'll be watching for that. No, we let him go for now."

"For now?"

Debbie was busy at the keyboard. "Got it."

"What?" asked Seline. "Got what?"

"His license plate number, for one thing. The cameras in the parking lot got that and the ones in here got a good read on his ID. We'll soon know if he's really FBI or not." She hummed to herself as she worked. Ellen poured Seline another coffee then one for herself. They retreated to the inner office to enjoy it. Debbie came in a few minutes later. "The guy's ID was a fake, of course, but I have another address to check out."

"Sit down, Debbie," said Ellen. "We need to brainstorm this thing."

The girl raised a finger, fled to the outer office, then returned with a coffee for herself. "Ready," she said, as she sank gracefully into a chair.

"Okay, let's look at this thing," said Ellen. "Mrs. Alldon came here this morning and this afternoon she's dead. I'd say she was followed here."

"Oh yeah," replied Debbie. "She was being watched. They really needed to know what we'd learned about Mr. Alldon."

"What did you give him?" asked Seline.

"Exactly what Ellen told him, and enough from the original files to make it real."

"Did you really delete the original?"

"Yes. You saw me do it and so did he."

"Have you already recovered them?" asked Ellen, a smile playing at her lips.

"Of course I have."

"I should have just grabbed him and beat it out of him, then tossed the body in the harbor," muttered Seline.

"Actually, I'm curious," said Ellen. "Why didn't you?"

"I didn't know what surveillance we have and who has access to it besides us."

"So, you read spy stories too?" asked Ellen.

"Once in a while," Seline replied. "So, what do we do now?"

"First, you did right, Seline. You do have good instincts. Yes, you didn't dare grab him here nor did we dare to follow him. However, we're not done by a long shot."

"Look, I don't want you guys getting involved, I ..."

"Too late for that now," said Debbie. "Mrs. Alldon got us involved without your help. I for one, don't want to end up like she did, just a loose end getting tied up."

"Nor do I," agreed Ellen. "So, what's our next step?"

"Well, I'll find him," said Seline. "It's my bet he'll try to follow us, or at least one of us."

"No," replied Ellen. "There are too many dead bodies lying around on this one already. No, I think we're safe enough, but I'm willing to bet we have a break in here tonight. We'll arrive in the morning to find the door pried open and all our computers smashed or missing."

"Not gonna happen," said Seline. Her eyes seemed to be focused far away. "So there you are, Agent Daniels. Lady Shadow will be waiting. She has questions for you, questions that need answers." She shook her head and allowed her vision to refocus on the room. "He's in an old car, halfway down the block. Not the same one he left in. When you guys leave for the day it'll look like I'm with you."

"But you'll still be here?" asked Debbie.

"Oh yeah, we'll be here."

"We?" asked Debbie.

"Me and a few friends," replied Seline. "You've met some of them already."

"Oh, those friends. All right then."

"Have you got a plan, Seline?" asked Ellen.

"You mean besides stopping him from wrecking the place?"

Ellen smiled. "Yes, besides killing him. Girl, we need information more than retribution."

"There's that *we* again."

"Seline, Mrs. Alldon brought us into this, not you. Like it or not, that man sees us as a loose end. I expect him to come charging in here with a squad of people, seize everything, and make us all disappear."

"Oh shit. What do we do?"

Ellen's jaw was set. "We have to turn the tables here. We need information, then he has to disappear. Whatever is going on here needs to stop. If enough of them start disappearing they'll shut down and go away."

"I don't like that idea," said Seline. "I need the guys at the top. I have to find them before they vanish."

"Then we need information, not bodies," said Debbie.

Seline nodded, her eyes going hard. "Got it. Information first. Dammit, I wish I knew what questions to ask. I was supposed to have a lot more training time before we got to this point."

"I could help you," suggested Ellen.

"Me too," said Debbie. "I want in."

Seline appeared to be thinking. "All right," she said at last. "At closing time he'll see the three of us lock up and leave. As soon as he breaks in, I'll take him in the outer office. You two stay in here until I call you to join us. After we have the information we need I'll take him away and make him disappear.

"Debbie, make sure all our surveillance is disconnected."

"Why?"

"Because we don't know who is tapped into it and we don't want any record of what will happen here," said Ellen.

"Right. Gotcha. Now, let's make a list of questions for Seline to ask him."

It had been a long, boring, afternoon of surveillance, but he was used to it. He'd done plenty of it over the years. Finally, as the sun set, he saw the three women emerge from the office, set the alarms, then get in their cars and drive away. He waited impatiently for them to disappear around the block then he slipped out of his car and into the shadows. A few moments later he disabled their alarms and jimmied the locks. He slipped inside, and then his world went all to hell.

The door closed behind him with a soft click. There was some illumination from the soft light filtered in from the streets, but he needed more. He flicked on a small flashlight that cast a tight beam across the room. Something moved in the shadows. He swept the light towards it, reaching for his gun. The beam of light landed on a writhing form, a king cobra. As he raised the gun the snake struck, its fangs sinking into his hand and sending both the gun and the flashlight to the floor.

His eyes were growing accustomed to the light now and he saw her, a female form moving with liquid grace. She stopped just out of his reach, smiling to show her elongated fangs. "The serpent's bite is poisonous. You will want this." She held up a small vial of liquid. "It's the antidote." He leaped at her, one hand grasping her wrist about the vial she held and the other tightening on her throat. She broke his grip easily and hurled him against a tree.

As a trained agent, he was prepared to remain calm in the face of the unexpected, but he was struggling. He was supposed to be in a room inside an office building in the city. He wasn't. He was in a boreal forest, the trees were small, the air cold, and the ground hard. He shivered as he struggled back to his feet. He watched in horror as the snake crawled to the woman, up her leg, around her waist, and then down her arm to become an ornate staff.

"Do not doubt your senses," she said, laughing at him. "I've brought you to another world, a place more suited to my needs."

"Give me the antidote. I can already feel the poison in my bloodstream. Help me."

"No, not yet."

"What do you want?"

"Information. Don't bother looking for your gun; we left it behind in that other world."

His eye continued to search, looking for anything he could use for a weapon. He had to get that vial away from her. "What do you want to know?"

"Let's begin with the reason the Browns were killed."

"Give me the antidote first."

She tossed the vial to him, and he trembled as he pulled out the stopper. "Drink it all, every drop. It will work within seconds."

Greedily he swallowed, holding the vial over his mouth and shaking every last drop onto his tongue. His head began to clear almost instantly and the fire in his veins subsided. He looked around, taking in what he could in the pale moonlight. He was definitely on a different world. The three pale moons in the sky told him that much. That, and he could sense things in the trees, watching, waiting ..."

"Feeling better?" He just nodded. "All right then, about the Browns."

"Classified."

"Classify this," she said, her eyes going hard and her voice sounding like stone being ground to dust. "Aeorth!"

The man's eyes bugged out in fear as the huge sinuous shape began to coalesce from the shadows. The dragon was the size of an elephant, and its blazing gaze was fixed on him. It threw back its head and roared, sending a gout of hellfire into the night sky. That long neck swung about, and the diamond-shaped head moved closer to him as he tried to melt into the boulder at his back.

"Speak or I'll feed you to Aeroth and seek information elsewhere. The Browns."

The blazing eyes of the dragon finally broke him. He lost control of his bladder and began to babble. "They weren't married. They were partners, low level agents. They were couriers, nothing more."

"Why have them killed?"

"They discovered what they were transporting."

"Which was?"

"Drugs, street drugs, tons of it."

"To what purpose?"

"To sell," he stammered, trying to edge away from the dragon.

"Why? You're government agents. Why are you selling drugs?"

"We have to. We need the money to fund black ops outside the country."

"Why kill Mrs. Alldon?"

"Alldon screwed up. He left a witness to the Brown's killing. Every time he tried to reach that kid she beat him. He actually died trying to finish her. His wife hired private detectives to follow him. I couldn't take the chance they'd learned about the operation. I shot her and took her files."

"Does your superior know of this?"

"Yes, I made a full report."

"What was his response?"

He tried to edge further away, but the dragon made a sudden move and blocked him. Whimpering he inched away. "She said to clean up the mess and shut down the op."

"Explain clean up the mess?"

"Make the P.I.s disappear and destroy their offices. Please, call him off."

"No." She seemed to be thinking, then something vaguely man like whispered to her. Finally she nodded. "What steps have you taken towards this end?"

"I sent a team to the detective's condo. They've probably got her by now. I was going to make sure I had all the files then set the offices on fire."

"Give me the name of this supervisor and a place where I can locate her."

He swallowed hard, but didn't speak. She gestured with her hand and the dragon took a step forward, flame dancing around its nostrils as it breathed, its baleful gaze boring into his. "Jessica Sacheck," he babbled. "She has an office in the government building. Please ..."

The woman waved her hand, and he was back in the detective's offices. His eyes agog, he watched as she faded into shadow. His sigh of relief was short lived as another figure moved from the shadows. Swallowing hard, he staggered back from this new apparition. It was a young woman dressed in battered military fatigues. Her eyes we cold as deep space and there was no emotion at all in her voice.

"For the murders of the Browns, the attempted murder of Lexa Condon, and the murder of Jenine Alldon, you will now face Justice." He tried to run, but she was on him in a heartbeat, powerful arms encircling his neck. A quick twist, a loud cracking sound, and he went limp in her arms, his neck broken. She let the body slip to the floor. "Justice is served." She stepped back into the shadows and disappeared.

As the last vision faded, Seline came back into view. She saw the two women watching through the partially open door to the inner office. "You guys get all that?"

"We got it," replied Ellen. "My god, Seline, that was so real, all of it. Who was that last one? She was so cold, she scared me more than the dragon."

"She's called Lady Justice. She lives in another city and fights injustice there. Moragah showed her to me once. I tried to get close to her as I could, but I've never met her so I can't be sure. Moragah says she goes cold when she dispenses justice. No emotion; not revenge, not compassion, nothing until well after it's over.

"Okay, we've got problems. I'll take care of the body. Ellen, you drive Debbie home. Make sure there are no agents waiting to make her disappear. Come back for me and we'll take care of the ones waiting for us at home. If they're at Debbie's place, bring her with you, we'll have a house guest for a while."

Ellen nodded. She and Debbie grabbed their coats, purses, and keys then left the building. They got in Ellen's car and watched as Seline came out with the dead body over her shoulder like a sack of grain. She tossed it into the back seat of Old Betsy and drove away. As soon as she vanished around the block they left for Debbie's apartment complex. There was no unwanted welcoming committee. Ellen dropped her off and returned for Seline.

"This is seriously creepy," Seline muttered to herself, as she drove towards the bridge over the inner harbor. "I'm driving through the city with a dead body in the car. A man I killed and not in self defense. I executed this guy just like they did the Browns." She shuddered, fighting to keep her focus on the road. "How does that make me better than them?"

The vast presence of Moragah engulfed her, easing her mind. "Be at peace, my daughter. You have done what I asked of you. Nothing more. Seline, death is not the end of the spirit's journey, just another passage to a different state of being. Had you questioned this man further, looked into his past, you would have found a number of murders. You would have found hundreds of destroyed lives as a result of the drugs he imported to sell.

"Seline, you have merely plucked a hair from the beast of darkness invading this world. As you search higher into his organization you will find darker and darker spirits in your path, and you will have to deal with them."

"Moragah, can you make me go cold, like Lady Justice, so I don't feel anything when I have to do this?"

"If I do that, you will truly become like them. Seline, I may have removed too much from Tasha. She was such a gentle soul, but so traumatized. In the end, I sent Kara to her to provide balance. It has worked well, and I'm pleased with them.

"I'm also pleased with you. The reach of your imagination is impressive, and you're just beginning to feel your power. That image of Tasha was perfect, right down to her usual method of dealing with the guilty."

"Then why do I feel so weird inside?"

"At first, Penny was almost physically ill after a battle. It is the same for all, even Tasha. I always have to make a few tweaks, as you say, at first. As you learn to use your abilities things change for you and I make gentle adjustments to help you with that.

"You've done well, Seline. I'm proud of you, my daughter. Remember your sense of fun and let Ellen help you."

She was at the bridge, so Moragah pulled back to let her work. The bridge was empty of traffic as it was now late at night. Seline stopped the car and got out. She pulled the body from the back seat and hurled it over the rail. It disappeared into the gathering fog below. With a sigh of relief Seline got back in, burned a u-turn and headed back to the office. She had only a few minutes to wait.

Ellen found the old car in the parking lot but no Seline, and then she stepped from the shadows. "I tossed the body off the bridge," she said, as she settled into the car with Ellen. "I got his car keys. His car is just down the block. I'll drive it back to the bridge and you follow me."

"That's a good plan. Be careful not to leave any fingerprints."

"Gotcha." Seline got out and walked back to the agent's car. She pulled her sleeve over her hand as she opened the door and settled inside. The trip back to the bridge was uneventful and she was grateful for that. She left it where she had thrown the body then got back in with Ellen. "Okay, let's go home and finish this."

"Are you up for that? We could get a hotel instead. Tonight must have taken the good out of you."

"It did, but I can still function. Oh, I reset the locks on the office."

"Great, thanks. Seline, that was something wild that you did, the other world thing."

"Yeah, he knew he had to talk to me if he wanted to get back. He played fair so I brought him back to face Justice."

"Yeah, wow. I hope I never meet her in person."

"Moragah says she's a sweetheart when she's not in combat mode, but she goes cold when the action starts. Okay, here we are. Just give me a minute to locate these guys."

She focused for a moment then found them just inside the underground parking garage. She listened for a minute and learned an agent Linwood was in charge. Seline opened her eyes then pulled out a strange cell phone from her pocket. She thumbed it on and hit contacts. A quick scroll turned up Linwood. She hit call then waited. When she spoke, it was in Daniels' voice. "Linwood, it's a bust. This op is called off. Go home and report to the office in the morning."

"Roger that," came the reply.

They waited for a minute, then a van exited the garage followed by two identical cars. Seline checked the garage again, then sighed deeply. "Take me home, Ellen. I'm fading fast here."

"Come on, Granny," said Ellen, as she took Seline's arm and steered her into the elevator. "Let Ellen help you."

"So that's how you want to play, is it? Fine." Seline suddenly changed her appearance and leaned heavily on Ellen's arm.

Ellen laughed with delight as she gently hugged the elderly woman leaning against her. "That's right, dearie. You just lean on Ellen, and I'll take you home then tuck you into bed."

"You could come with me," purred a deep sexy voice as Seline morphed into a tall, green-eyed redhead.

Just then, the elevator doors opened and Ellen pushed her through. She was laughing. "Get out, you perv."

Seline returned to herself as Ellen reached to unlock the door and it swung open at her touch. "Let me," said Lady Shadow as she stepped past Ellen. Ellen followed her in, gun in hand. The place had been ransacked. "Hold on. Let me make certain we're alone."

Ellen watched as the tall woman in the flowing robes closed her eyes. She opened them again a moment later. "We're alone, but there are several listening devices and two hidden cameras. I will disable them." She closed her eyes again. A moment later there were several sizzling pops from various locations. Lady Shadow faded back into Seline.

"Son of a bitch," swore Ellen, as she replaced her gun in her purse and tossed it onto the counter. Seline stepped over and easily righted the dining table, and then the couch. As she continued to straighten the furniture, Ellen began to take stock. "Doesn't look like anything is missing, but they tossed the library. It'll take a couple of days to set it right again."

"They buggered up the library? Okay, now I'm pissed off. This shit just got personal."

"Easy, girl, easy. You've already had a long day. Tomorrow is Friday. We can take the weekend off and set it right. I'm thinking a day or two of rest in the library is just what you need."

"Yeah, maybe you're right," sighed Seline, allowing her shoulders to droop. "I wonder what they were looking for?"

"They weren't looking for anything, this was a warning."

"I'll give them a warning they won't soon forget."

Ellen smiled in spite of the situation. "Come on, my fierce warrior woman," said Ellen, as she took Seline by the arm, "it's time to tuck you into bed."

"Be still my heart," grinned Seline.

Ellen laughed with delight. "You don't have the energy left for that and neither do I. Come on, Miss Naughty."

"Oh, I get it, you liked the red head better." Seline morphed into the redheaded girl again and started to strip off her clothes.

"Stop it, you fool," laughed Ellen. "Or else."

"Or else what?" asked Seline, as the last of her clothes fell to the floor. "What will you do, my delicious?"

Seline was expecting Ellen to run away, but she didn't. "Oh honey, I just might take you up on it," purred Ellen.

"Get out of my room, you perv," said Seline, as she stepped back and grabbed a pillow to cover herself with. She was laughing as Ellen stepped to the doorway. "Ellen, thanks."

"For?"

"Helping me to remember who I am."

Ellen smiled. "Go to sleep. I'll go reset the alarms and a few traps in case we have return visitors."

"If we do they'll be sorry," said Seline, as she dropped a nightie over her head and settled it on her body. Something huge stirred in the shadows. "You go on to bed. I'll leave Aeroth to watch through the night." The dragon came fully into view, a smaller version, rubbed gently against Ellen on his way out the door and down the stairs.

Ellen watched him go. "He's becoming quite real to you, isn't he?"

"He is real, and so is she."

"Seline, what is it?" Ellen stepped closer and pulled the girl into her arms. She was trembling.

"I'm scared, Ellen. I'm scared that she's becoming more real and I'm fading. Soon there won't be anything left of me at all."

"Oh, sweetie, that's the way it's supposed to be, isn't it? Clark Kent wasn't real, Superman was. Clark was just the illusion, Kal-el was the one who was real."

"So I'm not real, she is?"

Ellen held Seline by the shoulders and gazed into her eyes. "You *are* Lady Shadow. We constructed Seline together, remember? We made her to give you a way to move about in public, but you're really Lady Shadow. You're not being absorbed into the illusion, you're becoming more your true self. You're fighting it, that's why it takes the good out of you. You change your appearance at will because that's just a disguise anyway. It's always you in there and you are Lady Shadow. Stop resisting and become who you truly are."

Seline gazed into Ellen's eyes for a long moment as she absorbed what the woman had said. Finally she nodded and spoke softly. "That makes so much sense. Ellen, what would I have done without you?"

"Oh, you would have perished long ago," replied Ellen, grinning with mischief. "You need me."

Seline chuckled as Ellen stepped away. "Badness. Yes, I do need you. Thanks for putting me back together."

"Any time," replied Ellen as she reached the door.

"Ellen."

"Yes?"

"You can still have the redhead if you want," grinned Seline, as she morphed again.

"Go to sleep, perv," laughed Ellen as she stepped out and closed the door.

Seline changed back to herself and flopped back onto the bed. "She's right, isn't she, Moragah. I'm not really Seline, am I?"

"No, my priestess, you are Lady Shadow, and your powers are growing. I am actually surprised at what you can do."

"Sorry you made me?"

"Not at all. I am quite enjoying you, Shadow. It intrigues me how you will bring light back to the world through the use of shadows. Sleep now, and rest. I will watch over you, as will Aeroth."

"Is he truly real now?"

"He is as real as anyone else. Yes, your pet is real. Your creations will be solid or shadow as you desire. Sleep now."

Ellen descended the stairs to see the dragon resting in the living room. He had pushed aside the coffee table and overstuffed chair to make room. He raised his head as she walked by, nodded to her, then turned his attention to the doorway. Ellen smiled. Nothing would survive getting through that door tonight. As she crawled into her bed she marveled at how she had come to accept Seline's illusions as real.

Learning the Trade

E llen arrived at work the next morning to find Debbie waiting for her outside. "What's up?"

"I can't get in. Somebody did something with the locks."

"Somebody?"

"The locks were forced, but now they seem to be working fine, except my codes won't work."

Ellen grinned. "I left her sleeping it off. I'll bet she changed the codes when she fixed the locks."

"She's a locksmith, too?"

"Among her many talents, Lady Shadow is a whiz with locks," replied Ellen. "Let me see now, four digit combo. Hmmm. L-A-D-Y? Damn, it didn't work. Wait. L-E-X-A," the lock clicked open. "Yes."

"Lexa?" asked Debbie, as they entered and hung up their coats.

"Yes, that was her name when all this started. Lexa Condon. We changed it to Seline Elmore to get them off her trail."

"Hmm, didn't work. Pity that."

"Oh, it worked," replied Ellen, setting the coffee pot to brew. "They didn't track her to us. They came at us because the assassin's wife led them here."

"Coincidence?"

"Yep, just plain bad luck."

"Ellen, I get the impression these are government people. Can we survive this? Should we go public?"

The coffee pot wasn't quite ready, but Ellen's patience with it ran out. She whipped out the carafe, poured up two mugs, then set it back in the machine. "Normally, I would say yes, get the media all over it and keep them there."

Debbie gratefully accepted one of the mugs from Ellen's hand. She moaned with delight as she took her first long sip. "So, not this time?"

"Nope, not this time."

"I guess it would be hard to explain what happened to Agent Daniels."

"That and we don't want to attract attention to Seline."

"Yeah," chuckled Debbie. "We'd be pretty poor allies if we blew her cover in the first few days. However, that could leave us in a very dangerous position. Ellen, if this goes sideways..."

"I know."

"Ellen, why did we get involved in this? Oh, I know that Mrs. Alldon put us in the soup, but you were already mixed up in it, weren't you? Why? How?"

"How long have we been best friends, Debbie?"

"Since grade school when you beat up the bully who was picking on this poor little black girl."

"How long have I had that heart defect?"

"Since grade five. What has that got to do with all this?"

"I first met Seline in a hotel room rented by Mr. Alldon. I didn't know it then, but he was already dead. I was hidden, but she saw me. While we were sizing each other up, a guy came to execute Alldon. Seline used an illusion to make him think he had succeeded. We got out of there and we talked. She fixed me, Deb, at least her goddess did."

"Her goddess? Really? A goddess?"

"Yes, her goddess. Get that look off your face; I know how that sounds. The truth is, Seline met a goddess and was granted super powers. She asked for my help, and they fixed me." Ellen pulled open the file cabinet and passed a file to Debbie. It was her medical file. Debbie glanced at it, then looked closer. Her gaze returned to Ellen, her mouth open. "That's right, my sister in crime, they fixed me. I can't tell you how good it feels to walk down the street and not be imagining my own body lying dead with panicked strangers trying to revive me. I'm free for the first time since I was a child.

"Debbie, I owe Seline, you don't. You should run for your life, find another job..."

"Forget that, woman. You kept the bullies off me in school, you pulled my sorry ass back off the bridge when I tried to jump because Jim left me; I will not back away from you now. You've always had my back, and now I've got yours. I'm in, end of discussion. Besides, I own half this agency and you're not buying me out cheap."

Ellen smiled at her friend, then refilled the coffee mugs. The police arrived an hour later. Seline was right behind them.

Seline awakened to sunlight streaming through the windows. She stretched luxuriously, then rose to face the day. She stepped to the window and raised her arms towards the morning sun. "Great Lady Moragah, I thank you for my night's rest and for the awesome gifts you gave me. Thank you for this new day to enjoy. May all those of us who serve you be pleasing to you this day. May your name be revered and blessed."

"That was delightful, Seline," came Moragah's warm thoughts. She surrounded Seline with loving energy for a long moment.

Seline was smiling happily as she dressed and headed downstairs for breakfast. The dragon was still there, but sleeping. She stroked the long brow ridge affectionately, then went to the kitchen. "Oh shit!" The clock on the stove told her clearly how late she was; grabbing a banana, she bolted out the door. Seline exited the cab just as the police car arrived at the office. She and the officer entered the building together.

The officer introduced himself and asked about Mrs. Alldon. She'd been found dead in her home earlier, the agency's card on the table near her. Ellen told him about the case. When he asked for the files, she told him about Agent Daniels. He noticed the security cameras.

Debbie gave him a digital copy of the meeting with Agent Daniels and he went away happy.

"This is getting complicated," muttered Seline, pouring a mug of coffee.

"Actually, this could take the pressure off us for a while," said Ellen. "Think about it. They now have a tape of Agent Daniels in here, all hot and fussy about Mrs. Alldon's file. They now know that he knew she was dead when he arrived here yesterday, but he didn't report it. Now he's gone missing."

"So, this throws the attention back onto whatever agency Daniels was working for?" asked Seline. "How long will that last before they come looking for us again?"

"Couldn't tell you," replied Ellen. "It should buy us a few days at least. I'm hoping it might get us off the hook entirely."

"Talk to me, girl."

Ellen smiled as she replied. "This will start shining a lot of light in places that unknown agency wants to keep in the dark. I expect we'll soon have a visit from a stern faced agent warning us to stay away from this entire investigation."

"But we won't."

"Yes, my dear sorcerer's apprentice, we will. At least for a while. You still have lots to learn, things to practice, and we need to let the heat die down from this before we go trying to locate the next culprit on the ladder."

"Okay, but I'd like to locate that supervisor. What was her name? Jessica Sacheck?"

"Yes, that was the name," replied Ellen. "Debbie can locate the woman's office address for you, but we need to give it time before you make contact."

"All right, so what will I do for entertainment this afternoon?"

"You can see if you can tail this guy," laughed Debbie, as she passed a picture to Seline. "He's lost Ellen every time and Jack fared no better. He doesn't look like much, but he can spot a tail a mile away."

Seline was studying the photograph. "What's the deal with this guy?"

"His name is Henry," said Ellen. She passed a card to Seline with an address on it. "You can pick him up here. He's easy to spot, but murder to trail."

"And we're on his trail because?"

"His brother is in hiding and we're trying to serve him with divorce papers," replied Ellen. "I've wasted too much time on this guy already."

"Any idea how he got so good at spotting a tail?"

"He's a retired cop," said Debbie. "He usually sleeps all morning, but he'll be on the move soon. Just in case you get lucky, here's the summons. The target's name is George Hurley."

"Okay then, on my way." Seline caught the keys to Betsy that Debbie tossed to her as she left the building.

"Ten bucks says he loses her in the first two blocks," said Debbie, grinning.

"You're on," replied Ellen. "I'll also bet she comes back to report papers served."

"Oh yeah? What's the bet?"

"Loser buys pizza because I don't feel like cooking tonight."

"Deal. You're on."

Seline found the address easy enough. She sat for a moment thinking. "Okay, if he's ditched Ellen every time then he obviously knows this car. I should hide it. No, wait, I'll leave it here for him to see, but I won't be in it. Ellen will." There wasn't a lot of shade where she'd parked, but there was enough to form one image. As Seline blended with the people on the street the image of Ellen sat behind the wheel of the car, waiting.

A man dressed in a cheap suit came down the stairs and glanced about. She grinned as he spotted Ellen in the car. Jauntily, he sauntered down the street, keeping an eye on the car behind him. He looked slightly puzzled when the car didn't follow him. He stopped walking and glanced all around, checking every person on the street and every reflective surface he could find. No Ellen, but that kid with the cell phone set off his alarms. He walked into a menswear store.

Inside he inspected the racks nearest the windows. A young man followed him in, but the kid just walked by and got on a bus. He relaxed and returned to the street. A quick inspection showed no Ellen, no car, and no kid with cell phone. The young man who'd followed him into the store didn't come out. Satisfied he walked on.

He hadn't gone far when his senses began to set off the alarm again. He looked all around, but the street seemed to be clear. He continued. A short time later he spotted the kid with phone. She was behind him. Her reflection in the glass said she was following him. He ducked into the mouth of an alley. The kid walked past without a sideways glance, her attention on the phone. She was smiling to herself.

Seline's special vision showed her where Henry was hiding so she ignored him and continued on down the street. She'd used her special vision to see what he was doing when he spotted her following. She was keeping notes with her phone. Seline ducked around the next corner and morphed into a well dressed woman in a blue business suit. Henry walked by, his eyes searching everywhere for the kid with the phone and ignoring the woman with the briefcase. When he finally became aware of her she entered a ladies bra shop and a moment later an elderly woman leaning on a cane came out.

The cat and mouse game went on for several more blocks until Henry finally approached an older apartment building, spoke on the buzzer and was admitted. "Nice try," grinned Seline, as she approached and looked at the board. She began pushing all the buttons. "Hey, it's me. Let me in," she sang in a breathless voice when the buzzer was answered. Several ignored her, three swore at her, and finally one buzzed her in. Grinning wickedly, she pulled the door open and slipped inside. It took only a moment with her special vision to locate her quarry. She climbed the stairs to the second floor and approached the door of #23.

Seline pulled out the summons and held it behind her back. She morphed into a busty redhead showing lots of cleavage then tapped on the door. "Who's there?" asked a suspicious voice.

"Larry, it's Ginger. Let me in."

"There's nobody named Larry here. Go away."

"Aw come on, Larry, stop playing around and let me in. I know you're in there." Seline could hear someone on the other side of the door. "Larry, come on."

The door swung open, and a man stepped to block her path. It wasn't Henry. Seline started to step forward but stumbled against him. He caught her and stood her back up. "Thanks mister. Say, you're not Larry."

"That's what I've been trying to tell you. I'm not Larry."

"Gosh, I'm so sorry. I'm Ginger."

She started to offer her hand and he reflexively reached for it. "George, I'm George."

Instead of a warm hand he closed his fingers over a paper envelope. He glanced down at it then looked back up. The camera on her phone flashed as she took the picture of him holding the summons. "George Hurley, you've been served," she said in a soft sexy purr. Smiling, she turned and walked back to the stairs. He stood frozen for a moment as she disappeared down the stairs then he ran after her. He reached the bottom of the stairs and bolted through the door, knocking aside a teenager who was looking at her phone.

"Hey, watch it, moron," said the teenager as she regained her feet. George ignored her as he frantically searched the street for the redhead. She was gone. Swearing profusely, he turned back and entered the building. Grinning, Seline e-mailed the photo to Debbie's computer back at the office then hailed a cab.

A tired Seline walked through the office door to find Ellen and Debbie feasting on pizza. Grabbing a slice for herself, she sank onto the sofa and kicked off her shoes.

Ellen was grinning at her. "So you managed to trail Henry; I am impressed."

"Yep, and I served the papers, too. Do I get a bonus?"

"You get extra pizza and I forgive you for the dragon ripping the carpet in my office."

Seline sighed elaborately and winked at Debbie. "I'll take it." She reached for another slice.

Dead End

It took all weekend to put the library back to rights. Late Sunday afternoon Ellen declared it finished, then they each chose a book and curled up in a chair to read. An hour later Seline realized Ellen was watching her. "What?" she asked as she made eye contact.

"You've got friends," replied Ellen, indicating Seline should look over her shoulder.

Seline turned to look. There were three faeries floating lazily behind her, looking over her shoulder, a heavily armed dwarf sat on the floor smiling and caressing the fur of a huge wolf. Seline tilted her head and gave them all an exasperated look. Ellen could hear the faeries giggling as they all faded back into the shadows. "Sorry."

"Just don't bring Aeroth in here; he's too big and he'll wreck the place again."

Seline just chuckled and went back to her book. It had been far too long since she'd taken the time to just sit and read. She gently closed the book and lowered it to her lap. "Lady Moragah."

"*I am here, Seline, my daughter.*"

"Thank you for this short time of peace."

"*You need this, my priestess. This restores you and empowers you. Take this time to allow your imagination to stretch, to absorb the possibilities of what you will become.*"

"Am I to be a hero in a book? Not real to the rest of the world?"

"*No, you will be real both as the shadow weaver and as the woman. This is a difficult time for you, Seline. More difficult for you than for the others. Seline, you are unique among the priestesses and will be the most*" *powerful of them all, for yours is the more dangerous task. It will take time for you to grow into your strength and become comfortable with it. Relax and allow yourself to enjoy who you are, who you are becoming."*

"Thanks, Moragah. I'll admit it, I had fun trailing that man the other day. He was really good, and I learned a lot."

"Oh, such as?"

"He was always so aware of his surroundings. I need to practice that."

Seline felt the wave of loving energy as the presence of Moragah enveloped her. *"I'm quite proud of you, my priestess of shadows. Rest now and enjoy your book."* Seline closed her eyes and basked in Moragah's energy for a moment until the goddess pulled back. Smiling, she returned to her book. A moment later she glanced at Ellen and grinned.

By the oddest chance, Ellen glanced up from the page and caught that grin. "Seline, there had better not be an alien spider sitting on my shoulder." Seline's grin just widened. Slowly, carefully, Ellen lowered her book and turned. There, on the back of her chair, sat the red haired girl, dressed in a slinky green dress. She smiled, licked her lips, and winked at Ellen. Ellen sighed elaborately and shook her finger at Seline, who giggled and let the image fade.

The weekend of relaxation and reading did them both good and they were well rested when they arrived at work on Monday. One glance at Debbie's face told them all was not well. Ellen took morning report from the other investigators, handed out the new assignments, then called Debbie and Seline into the inner office. "Okay, Deb, out with it. What's gone sideways on us now?"

"I spent much of the weekend searching for this Supervisor Jessica Sacheck."

"And?" asked Seline.

"Dead, according to the news report," replied Debbie. "Supposedly she was hit by a drunk driver while out for a run."

"Well, isn't that convenient," sighed Ellen. "So, now the question is, is this a cover up for another murder or is it a cover story while she gets moved to a new job with a new name?"

"No," said Debbie. "The question now is, do we care? Either way this signals we're out of the fire, right?"

"I believe you're right, Deb," replied Ellen. "Whatever the reason, this woman disappearing from our lives signals the heat is off. If they were still planning to come at us, it would be her trying to clean it all up. This tells me whoever they are, they've decided to shut this down and remove themselves from the potential spotlight. I believe we can breathe easier; we've probably heard the last of this."

"Thank god for that," sighed Debbie. Suddenly her coffee mug stopped midway on its journey to her lips. Her eyes opened wide as she glanced at Seline who had barely spoken a word. Seline was no longer there, the Shadow Elf was.

Ellen still hadn't noticed the change in her friend. "Seline, you haven't said much. What do you ...?" Her voice trailed off as she saw the tall woman clad in leather armor rise and begin to pace about the room.

"This news is disturbing to me," came that rich contralto voice. "It means we've lost the trail." She clenched her fist tightly for a moment, then deliberately flexed her long fingers. "It means they have escaped me. For now." She stopped pacing and turned to face her companions. "Ah well, they are what they are, they will cross my path again. In the meantime, my alter ego needs to sharpen her skills." She resumed her seat and, with a visible effort to concentrate, morphed back into Seline once again.

Debbie finally managed to get a sip of the coffee, then returned the mug to the desk. "You might want to work on that a bit."

"Work on what?" asked Seline.

"Work out who you really are, the shadow warrior or Seline."

"I'm Lady Shadow; Seline is the disguise."

"Then you need to work on holding your form in disguise mode," said Debbie. "You got pissed and slipped into warrior mode on us."

"Sorry. Thing is, I can think so much more clearly when in warrior mode. Can you give me a minute; I need to confer with Moragah." She closed her eyes and took a deep breathe. "Lady Moragah?"

"I am here, my priestess."

"You heard?"

"I did."

"What should I do?"

"As you have already said, sharpen your skills and be patient. Those you seek will cross your path again. When they do, you will be far better prepared to face them. Patience, my warrior priestess, they will come to you again."

Seline thanked Moragah then opened her eyes. "Looks like we have some time to breathe. I'll keep an eye out, but for now we seem to be off their radar, and we've lost their trail. For now we go on with business as usual while I continue to learn the ropes and sharpen my skills. Next time we butt heads with these people I want to be ready."

Ellen smiled and nodded. "I like that plan, but what makes you so sure they'll come at us again?"

"Me," replied Seline, "they'll come at me. They're government, governments are always meddling, so they'll cross my path sooner or later. When they do, I want to be ready. Next time I'm hoping to keep you guys out of it."

Things were fairly quiet for several weeks. Seline spent her days on more mundane jobs, following wayward husbands, finding runaway kids, and tracking down a few bail jumpers. She honed her investigations skills by day, and by night she worked on her otherworldly talents. She was far faster now, and could follow a conversation from two blocks away while on a dead run. Her extra vision was clearer, and she could switch back and forth between extra vision and normal in the blink of an eye.

She could also switch between Shadow the elf warrior and Seline the detective in an instant. She began to go out at night hunting for drug dealers, using her speed and strength to subdue them, and only changing to Shadow to interrogate them. She was saving her illusions for bigger fish. However, she didn't neglect her power of illusion. She practiced that as well. Aeroth could flicker between solid and shadow at will.

One night Ellen found her in the library, a wolf at her feet and a young dragon on her shoulder. "Hey there, I didn't expect to find you home so early. Everything okay?"

Seline closed the book and looked up. There were tears in her eyes. "I did something terrible, Ellen."

Ellen was instantly on the arm of the chair gathering Seline into her arms. "Tell me," she breathed softly into the girl's hair. Her eyes opened wide as Seline morphed into Lady Shadow. She felt the rough wool of the woman's tunic and heard the creak of the leather armor as Shadow stood up, her arm around Ellen's waist, bringing her to her feet as well.

Still holding Ellen to her side, Shadow waved her arm through the air and the scene changed. They were on a city street, outside a coffee shop. "Observe." Ellen watched as Seline's adventure played out before her.

Seline came out of the coffee shop to find a small boy standing by her car. He looked to be about seven or eight years old, and he had a note pinned to his shirt. "I'm lost," he said, as she approached. "Can you help me get home?" He pushed out the note for her to read.

Seline crouched down and read the scrawled note. "Billy, is that you name?" The note just had his name and an address on it.

"Yes. This is where I live. Will you take me home?"

Seline's warning instincts were jangling, but her maternal instincts were stronger. "Sure. Hop in." She opened the car door for him.

The address turned out to be in a bad part of town, but the house did have two newer cars parked out front. The house itself was quite rundown showing both neglect and abuse. Billy insisted she come inside to meet his dad, so she reluctantly got out of the car. Halfway to the door her warning senses finally gained control. She stopped walking and let her special vision check things out.

The boy was trying to pull her along by the hand. "Come on, lady. My dad wants to meet you."

Step by slow step he dragged her towards the door while her vision explored inside. She saw several young men, mostly still in their teens, laughing and drinking. Two of them held a woman down, slapping at her face while a third raped her. Their buddies watched and cheered them on. A second woman lay on the floor in a pool of blood, her clothing, obviously expensive, torn and shredded. She was weeping quietly and trying to crawl away. The boy tugging on Seline's hand was unaware as she shifted into the shadow warrior.

The door swung open and hands reached for her. "Get your ass in here, bitch." She grabbed the reaching hand and yanked hard. Pulled off balance the youth staggered towards her. He met her fist coming the others way. His jaw shattered under that blow and his neck snapped. As the body fell to the floor she leaped past it.

For a moment the gang just stared at the apparition in the room. She was tall, her mass of red hair pulled back in a thick braid. Her body was clothed in well worn leather armor that bore the blood stains of battles long past. Short spikes adorned her boots and gloves. She snarled showing long canine fangs and the rage that burned in her emerald green eyes sent shivers through them.

"What the fuck are you?"

"I'm Lady Shadow. You're all going to die." She suddenly moved. The man who'd been raping the woman was swept high into the air then smashed head first into the floor, killing him instantly. A gun was aimed at her but she grabbed one of the men holding the woman down and dragged him into the line of fire. He took several bullets before she hurled the body into the gang, knocking several to the floor. She blurred out of sight.

Moving too fast for the eye to follow, she fought them. They tried to bring guns and knives to bear, but all to no avail. Her powerful blows first ripped and tore at flesh and her kicks broke bone as she maimed them before killing them. It was utter carnage as she tore through them, a savage avenging, and pitiless demon.

When all were down she came back into sight, breathing deeply. The small boy was still there, trying to bring a gun to bear on her. She batted it aside then grabbed him by the scruff. With a snarl on her perfect lips, she tore a blood stained shirt from a corpse and bound him with it.

"Who are you?" asked the woman who'd been brutalized. The woman who'd been on the floor was no longer moving. The woman who spoke was trying to hide herself behind a chair.

"You may call me Shadow," she replied, as she finished tying and gagging the child. "Can you walk?"

"I think so," she replied, levering herself upright. She shuddered as she looked at the still woman on the floor. "They killed her. They raped and beat her to death. I was forced to watch and then it was my turn."

"Do you know why they did this?" asked Shadow, as she dropped the boy to the floor.

"It's a gang initiation. The child has to lure a woman here to be raped and beaten to death. When they achieve that, they're in the gang." She began to shudder and weep as she tried to pull the remnants of her clothing about her.

"Can you find your things? Do you have the means to call the police and ambulance?"

"Yes, I think so."

"Then do so. When they ask, tell them Lady Shadow is now in the city. I won't tolerate this. There will be many dead from the gang that began this custom, before I'm through." Shadow faded into mist right before the woman's eyes.

The scene faded and Ellen was back in the library, still held in Shadow's arms. Shadow slowly morphed back into Seline who burst into tears and buried her face on Ellen's shoulder. "Oh god, Ellen, I wanted to kill that kid so bad, too," she sobbed. "And I should have. How much damage will he do when he grows up?"

"Hush now, Seline, Ellen's got you," soothed Ellen. "You couldn't kill a child and that's as it should be. He could grow up to become a doctor, you never know."

"Most of the others were just kids," said Seline, as she sniffed and stilled in Ellen's arms.

"They were old enough to know what they were doing. They paid for their crime and I'm not one bit sorry for them, nor should you be. As the saying goes, they've reaped what they've sown."

"I guess." Seline leaned back to look into Ellen's eyes for a long moment. "This is the part where you take advantage of my vulnerable state and kiss me."

A smile teased at Ellen's mouth as she pulled Seline a little tighter. "Darn, I nearly missed the cue," she breathed, as she brought her lips to Seline's.

The kiss was soft and sweet. Seline moaned as their lips parted and laid her head on Ellen's shoulder. "Like kissing your sister, huh?"

Ellen chuckled softly. "I wouldn't know, I never had a sister. It didn't start your engine either, did it?"

"It was really nice, but..."

Ellen squeezed her tighter for a moment. "Okay, we've got that out of the way now. How about I mix us up an Irish Coffee to chase the blues away?"

"Deal, sweet sister."

They were barely settled in the library with their drinks when the door buzzer sounded. Ellen went to answer it then returned with a policeman in tow. "Seline, this is Police Detective Walsh. He has some questions for us. All right, officer, ask away."

The policeman was young and a bit shy. He blushed as he cleared his throat then spoke. "Ladies, you are the owners of the Cameron Detective Agency, correct?"

"Ellen is, I just work there."

He made a note in his book. "Ladies, a car registered to your agency was reported to be at the scene of a mass murder this afternoon."

"That was me," said Seline.

"What were you doing there?"

"I picked up what I thought was a lost child. He had an address pinned to his shirt and asked me to take him home. When I saw the neighborhood I got nervous, let him out of the car and drove away."

"Ma'am, we found a child in that house, tied up hand and foot with blood soaked rags. The neighbors said your car was there for several minutes. They say it was there when they heard gunshots. Care to try again?"

"You wouldn't believe me if I told you."

"Try me."

Seline sighed then took another sip of her drink. Ellen was shaking her head, eyes wide in warning. Seline shifted her gaze back to the detective. "All right officer. The boy insisted I meet his dad and I followed him to the house. When the door opened I was grabbed and dragged inside. There were men there. Some were raping and beating a woman. There was another woman on the floor. I think she was dead. Before anything could be done to me something appeared in the room.

"It looked like a woman dressed up for one of those fantasy conventions, but it wasn't human. She started killing the men. I just crouched by the door until it was over. She told us to call the police and an ambulance, but I ran instead. You don't look surprised."

"The other woman told us a similar story. She didn't mention you, but her story was pretty sketchy. Her story of the creature doing the killing matches yours, though. Can you tell me anything more about the creature?"

"She said her name is Shadow. She was pretty pissed about what they did and said she'd find the rest of the gang and kill them too. I think she meant it."

"Shadow, that checks. Look, I have no idea what you really saw, or what you did, but I doubt you could have killed all those armed men by yourself. The other woman was in no shape to have helped you either. Whatever killed those men is extremely dangerous, and I don't like the idea of it running loose in this city."

"But you're all right with what that gang was doing?" asked Ellen, arching an eyebrow at him.

"No, ma'am, I'm not, but there's a right way and a wrong way to deal with these things. We can't have a vigilante prowling the city killing innocent citizens."

"Innocent?" Seline was on her feet and nose to nose with him. "There was only one innocent killed in that house today. It was the poor woman raped then beaten to death. Believe me, the rest weren't innocent. If Lady Shadow cleans out the lot of them I won't mourn a single one."

The policeman backed away from the fury in her eyes. "I didn't say that, ma'am. I just meant that this is a matter for the police."

Seline turned away and resumed her seat. "Forgive me if I disagree with you, officer. Without Lady Shadow's intervention I'd be dead or worse right now. I'm rooting for her. Oh, if you ever do meet her, don't piss her off."

"I'll bear that in mind. Thanks for your time, Ladies. I can see myself out."

Ellen followed him to the door anyway then reset the locks. She poured them each another drink and they settled down for the evening, but before long Seline put her book down. "He's coming back."

"Who? The policeman?"

"Yes. He thinks we're hiding something. He has another one with him. This one is going to play bad cop. He's planning to use threats, put the fear of god into us. They're outside in the car right now."

Ellen sighed. "Just stay calm, let me handle these guys." Seline nodded then took her book and moved to a bigger chair deeper into the room. She curled up, waiting. Ellen let them ring the bell several times before she answered. "What is it?"

"This is the police. Open up."

"No."

"Open the door, Lady. We just want to ask you a few questions."

"We've already answered your questions."

"We have a few more now open the damned door."

"Do you have a warrant?"

"I don't need a damned warrant now open the fucking door before I kick it in."

Ellen stepped back and put her phone to her ear as she unlocked the door. The big policeman brushed past her and swaggered into the living room. "All right, which one of you is the perp?"

"You mean the witness, don't you?" asked Ellen. "Seline, don't say a word until Robert gets here."

"Who the hell is Robert?" asked the big cop.

"My attorney," replied Ellen. "Once he arrives he will supervise the interview."

"The hell he will. I'm not wasting time waiting for no damn lawyer. Lady, you either start answering questions or we can do this downtown, and you can kiss your P.I. license goodbye."

At that point the young officer approached Seline who was cowering in her chair. "Ma'am, please, I just have a couple more questions."

She didn't answer. She just shrank deeper into the chair. Eyes wide with fear she pointed at the opposite corner. The officer glanced to where she was pointing, then took a step backwards. Something moved in the shadows. He reached for his gun, but Seline's fearful voice stopped him. "Don't! Guns just make her mad." His hand froze in the air above the weapon.

The other officer whipped out his gun and pointed it towards the shadow in the corner. The shadows deepened, moving, slowly coalescing into form. Suddenly a huge snake shot from the shadows right at the big policeman. He tried to bring his gun to bear but he was far too slow. The snake buried its fangs in his thigh and he screamed in fear and pain, dropping the gun to the floor. He was now face to face with a king cobra. It flared its hood and hissed at him.

A woman stepped from the shadows, tall, inhumanly beautiful with up-swept ears and fangs that showed with the smile that did not reach her eyes. She was dressed in blood stained leather armor and a thick braid of red hair fell across her shoulder. She made a hissing sound and the snake turned to strike at her. She caught it easily and it turned into a staff with a carved snake head.

Reaching out with the staff she lightly tapped the man's leg where the snake had bitten him. He hissed in pain and drew away from her. She used the staff to flick his fallen gun across the room to land beside Ellen. "The venom is swift, is it not?" she asked, her eyes boring into his. She passed him a small vial. "This is the antidote. Drink it all."

He eyed it suspiciously, finally accepting it with shaking hands. "Already your vision grows dim. Your time for choosing grows short. Drink or die; I care not which." With that she turned and stepped towards the younger policeman. Behind her, the other man drank every drop of what she had given him. She dropped the staff which once again became the cobra. It reared up to watch the big policeman carefully.

The young man eyed her cautiously. He could see she wasn't human, and he was having trouble meeting the penetrating gaze of those emerald green eyes. "Why did you return?" she asked. "This woman answered all your questions. Why did you return to threaten her?"

He swallowed hard, hoping his voice wouldn't betray his fear. "I made no threats."

"That is true, as it stands. However, you accompany the one who has made threats. Is this what you call police work, to abuse the victim instead of confronting the villains?"

"What do you mean?"

"You know full well who caused this afternoon's adventures. You know why those men did what they did. You know who caused them to do it. You also know they will continue, yet here you are, harassing one of the victims. Look at her. She was traumatized by those men and by witnessing me dispatch them."

"So, you admit you killed those men," said the older cop, as he regained his feet.

"I did, and with these weapons," she held up her hands to show the blood stained spikes on her gloves. "Those men brutalized those women. They faced the same fate; first I maimed them, then I killed them. That fate awaits all the members of that gang. When I find them, they will die in pain."

"You actually believe you can take down the whole gang?"

"Just watch me. Aeroth!" Something new moved in the shadows. A large serpentine form moved with alarming speed as it came fully into the room. The beast was heavily armored in glittering scales and its breath was dancing flames. The woman leaped easily to its back. "Get out there and do your job. Find and stop that gang before I find them. Harass these people any further and I will hunt you down." The dragon turned and leaped at the shadows playing along the wall. Beast and rider disappeared.

The big cop looked back, and the cobra was gone as well. With trembling hand he accepted the gun Ellen passed to him. "Any further questions?" she asked. He just turned and left. As he walked away she noticed he had wet himself.

The younger cop turned to Seline. "You called her, didn't you?"

"Yes," she replied, not meeting his eyes.

"Why?"

"Because I knew you wouldn't let it go. I knew you'd come back and threaten us. Whatever it is you want me to tell you, I don't know what it is."

"Can you contact her any time you want?"

"That depends on her. She promised to watch out for me for a few days, but that's all."

"What is she? Where did she come from? Why is she here?"

"I don't know. Why don't you ask her yourself the next time you see her?"

"So, you think I'll see her again?"

"Do your job and you might. You know what she's going to do. If you go after that gang you might bump into her again. Look, I can't help you. You have no reason to push me around; I didn't do anything wrong. I just gave a kid a ride home."

"Yeah, you're right. Miss Elmore, I am sorry. I won't bother you again. Good night, ladies. Sorry for the intrusion."

As the police left Ellen called her attorney back to save him the trip. As she closed the connection she noticed Seline standing in the kitchen, trying to reach the wine, but she was shaking too hard. "Let me." She guided Seline to a chair then poured wine for them both. "Tell me."

"It was the big cop. My dad was like that, a heavy handed bully. I was always terrified of him. Was I too hard on him, Ellen?"

"Oh hell no. He had that coming and more."

"Will he pull your license?"

"He can try, but I doubt he will. It's not all that easy to do, and besides, he embarrassed himself here. He won't ever want to see us again. Come on, honey, bring your wine and come back to the living room with me."

She took Seline by the hand and led her back to her chair. She lowered the lights, leaving Seline's lamp for reading and another for herself, but creating plenty of shadows as well. Seline picked up her book, but still seemed a bit rattled. "Seline, talk to Moragah then bring Aeroth back to keep watch. I think I want all the bases covered tonight."

Seline nodded her agreement then closed her eyes. "Moragah?"

"I am here, my priestess. You are troubled."

"I am. That man scared me. Ah, the truth is, I scared myself. Moragah, the way I killed those men. I hurt them first. That makes me no better than them."

"In what way?"

"I tortured and killed. It makes me feel sick inside."

"Did you take pleasure in the torture? In the killing?"

"No. It just made me feel sick inside."

"Then you are nothing like them. They derived pleasure from the screams of the tortured and they enjoyed the killing. You had to make an end of them, Lady Shadow, for had you not, they would continue, and many more innocents would suffer. Be at peace now, my daughter, and I will ease your distress." The vast presence of the mother goddess enveloped Seline, filling her with wellbeing and easing her mind. *"Much that you were forced to learn and absorb in childhood has no more value to you. It will only hinder you in your task. Let it go, Shadow. Allow yourself to become who you truly are."*

"Moragah, who am I now? I'm not who I was, but I don't know who I am, who I am supposed to be."

"You are Lady Shadow, priestess of Moragah, Goddess of Wisdom and Defender of the Weak. That is who you are. You are the guardian of the weak, the abused and helpless. You are the sheepdog who protects the flock from predators. You were taught that all life is sacred, and it is, at the

beginning. However, when a person decides to abuse and victimize others, they give up that sacred trust. They become the predators. Your task is to stop them, Shadow.

"Death is not the end of the spirit's journey, merely a passage to the next experience. Do not mourn those lives you have taken, rather, take joy in the lives you have saved." With another wave of loving energy, Moragah drew back.

Seline sighed with relief, her mind at peace. "Aeroth," she called softly. The dragon appeared from the shadows and came to her. She rubbed that diamond shaped head affectionately. "Be a dear and keep guard tonight?"

The beast gave a soft rumbling purr then turned towards the door. He paused to nuzzle at Ellen for a moment then settled down, his glittering eyes fixed on the door. Nothing would get past him, and Seline relaxed fully at last. With a sigh of contentment she opened her book and snuggled deeper into the chair. Ellen smiled as she watched Seline slowly morph into Shadow, dressed in a long green gown this time, no armor.

Changes

Over the next two weeks Seline spent more time as Lady Shadow than she did as Seline. Ellen and Debbie were beginning to notice changes in her, as Seline. Her hair which had been a honey blonde was turning red, she had freckles on her nose where none had been before, and her confidence was soaring, even as Seline.

Moragah had switched off much of the influence and thought processes her parents had imposed on her as a child. She still had a strong sense of justice, right from wrong, and a natural compassion for her fellow man, but she had lost all patience and compassion for those who chose to cross the line. Several more gang members were found dead, and the rest had gone into hiding.

Detective Victor Walsh had been following the exploits of Lady Shadow. There was a statewide warrant out for her arrest on a charge of murder and he was assigned to the case. He had tried following Seline Elmore, but that had proved fruitless. She lost him easily every time, and twice he had noticed her trailing him. He gave that up and moved to watching the gang leaders. It took him a while to find one of them, but he did.

A man known only as Ronaldo was holed up in a house, surrounded by a dozen heavily armed men. Men were seen coming out in threes and fours and returning with food and women, but Ronaldo himself was never seen. Half a block away an old man sat sleeping on the porch of an abandoned house, a hat pulled over his eyes. Suddenly every instinct he had screamed at him that he was in danger. He forced himself to remain still.

The figure that appeared in the shadows beside him sighed deeply then spoke. "So, the coward will not come out?"

"Lady Shadow, good to see you again," he said, once he regained control of his voice.

"And you, Officer Walsh."

"It's Detective Walsh, actually. Why are you here?"

"You've been looking for me, have you not?"

"Yes."

"Why?"

"Because you're a wanted felon, that's why."

"Explain."

"You've been murdering people. That's against the law."

"The men I have killed are also killers. They prey on the innocent. I hunt the predators. Why do you not hunt them?"

"We do."

"Then why are you out here when you know your quarry is in that house?"

"I'm out here gathering information. I can't go after them on my own; they're too heavily armed and there are too many of them. That would be suicide."

"And yet you hunt me. Be assured, I'm far more dangerous that the men in that house. Any attempt to capture or harm me will bring certain death."

He sighed and allowed his body to relax. "I believe you."

"Well then, shall we attack together?"

"What??? No, I..."

"You are afraid to face superior numbers."

"What? No. I mean, yes, that would be foolish, but it's not fear that..."

"What then? What holds you back from destroying these abusers?"

"Ronaldo is in there. I'd like to take him alive."

"Who is Ronaldo and why keep him alive?"

"He's the gang leader, the man in control. I want him alive so he can be brought to trial."

"Trial? You mean to have him face his accusers before answering for his crimes?"

"Yes. That's how the system works. That's the right way to do this. If you just kill them you're no better than they are."

"So you keep them alive to continue to spread their poison. You are content to make women like Seline Elmore have to face the man who hurt them. You would have them sit in a box and be accused of inviting the torture by those defending the abuser. You call this justice?"

"Everyone has the right to a defense."

"In my world they have a right to defend themselves. If we attack that house they will defend themselves against us. If they win they are free until another is sent against them. If not they have paid for their crimes and can harm no others. My way is better."

Detective Walsh swallowed hard and tensed. "I can't let you do that."

"You cannot prevent me. Truly, you would defend those within against me? Are your values so warped that you would risk your life for this?" He didn't respond. "Hmmm, all right, there is an alternative that will allow you to remain alive. Oh, you should relax. Your tension is concerning to my friend."

For the first time he noticed the cobra coiled up beside her. It reared up and flared its hood, fastening its gaze on him. He forced himself to relax his posture. "What's the alternative and what will it cost me?"

"I will help you capture this Ronaldo alive. In return, you will help me find the trail of an enemy that I have lost. I believe your connections within the police will be better suited to putting me back on the scent."

"You're after someone else?"

"Oh yes. Your little gang of petty thugs is no more than a distraction. And I'll confess, I've vented some frustration on them. I don't like losing track of my quarry."

"Who're you looking for?"

"You may know of the case. There were two people murdered in an apartment. A few days later another man was found dead in the next apartment. The trail went from there to a woman who was murdered, then to the murderer who threw himself off a bridge."

"I know the case. The man in the water was dead long before he hit the drink. His body was thrown off the bridge."

"Yes, well, I didn't think that would fool you for long. Anyway, most of these people were government agents. Their supervisor was killed before I could question her. So they say, but I believe she has just been relocated. I need to find her. I will deliver a live Ronaldo to you in exchange for helping me locate this woman."

"Look, that case is closed, and the file sealed. I can't go poking into that."

She surged to her feet, adjusting the weapons belt at her side. "Then I cannot help you either. I have work to do; just don't get in my way."

"Wait, please. All right; I'll see what I can find out. Look, Ronaldo is connected to some serious drug importers. We need to know what he knows, that's why I want him alive."

"You should have said this at the beginning. This is the information you thought to gain from Seline Elmore? How was she supposed to know anything about this?"

"She might have overheard something at that house, she might be one of the gang's girlfriends. She wasn't hurt and the other woman denied she was there. Maybe she was afraid Elmore would bring the gang down on her again."

"The men of your species are so amazingly stupid. So, we are agreed. In exchange for a live Ronaldo, you will help me?"

"Yes, it's a deal."

"Do you have some way for me to identify this Ronaldo?"

"Here."

He pulled a photograph from his pocket and passed it to her. She studied it for a long moment then returned it to him. "Watch from here, but don't try to interfere. I'll bring Ronaldo to you."

With that she stepped back into the shadows. He nearly wet himself as he heard her call the dragon. "Aeroth, come to me."

The beast appeared from the shadows, its scales gleaming in the fading daylight. She climbed easily to its back, then it gathered itself and leaped into the sky. Suddenly, with a scream of primal rage it dropped from the sky towards the house hiding the gangsters. The dragon swooped down, fire erupted from its mouth and engulfed the house. As the dragon landed the people inside the burning house ran outside.

One look at Aeroth and they scattered, their guns forgotten. Once again the beast leaped into the air. With a tight banking turn, Aeroth bore down on one fleeing figure and scooped it up in his jaws. He landed right in front of the policeman and spat out his prize. Shadow leaped from the dragon's back and grabbed the man by the collar. "What is your name?"

He began to babble so she thrust him towards Aeroth who snorted fire. "Ronaldo Garcia! My name is Ronaldo Garcia."

She hurled him to the ground at the policeman's feet. "He's yours, Detective Walsh. I've fulfilled my part of the bargain. When you have completed your part, contact Seline Elmore. She will know how to reach me." With that she climbed back onto her steed, and they disappeared into the evening sky.

While Ronaldo was being hauled away, the other gang members began to return. Lady Shadow stepped out of the bushes and, as they brought their guns to bear, they met their fate. She had kept her bargain, but these men were not part of the deal. They paid for their crimes and brutality in kind.

Three days later, Seline and Ellen arrived at the office to find Detective Walsh waiting for them. He and Debbie were chatting as they arrived. Ellen and Seline poured up coffee then took the detective into the inner office. Ellen settled back in her chair and indicated that he should sit facing her. "So, Detective Walsh, what can I do for you this time?"

"Actually it's Lady Shadow I've come to see," he said, turning to smile at Seline. "You said the males of our species are stupid, but I'm smart enough to figure out that you're Lady Shadow. That's why the other woman doesn't remember you being at that house. That's also why you're the only one who can contact her."

"You're not as smart as you think you are," said Ellen. "You've just sealed your fate."

"Wait, hear me out. Shadow, I think I have what you need."

Seline had already morphed into Lady Shadow. "Tell me."

"I took Ronaldo in, as agreed. I was immediately relieved from the case. The DA and detective sergeant questioned him for hours then some big shots with fancy credentials arrived. I was able to get close enough to overhear most of what they said. Ronaldo agreed to testify in exchange for immunity, but the big shots spirited him away. After listening to him confess some of what he did and was doing I regretted stopping you from killing him. He's already back on the street, recruiting for his gang."

He was somewhat surprised at her next question. "Tell me what you think happened."

"I think this guy is connected to somebody who can pull strings in high places."

"Tell me your suspicions."

"I have no proof of anything."

"Tell me anyway."

"I can't prove it, but I believe those men who sprung Ronaldo are CIA. We've known for years the CIA is bringing drugs into the country to finance some of their offshore activities. We've never been able to prove it. About that case you mentioned, the guys at the precinct believe that was a botched CIA operation."

"I do agree, but I fail to see how this helps me."

"I have a name. One of the big shots. Also, Ronaldo is on the loose again. If we track him you can question him before you kill him."

"You no longer have reservations about killing him?"

"What I heard him confess to sickens me," he said, not meeting her eyes. "The man is the worst kind of vermin, and the women and children of this city will be far safer with him dead."

"Is that why you're truly here, Detective Walsh?" asked Ellen. "Are you here hoping Lady Shadow will punish a man who the system protects?"

He sighed and gazed around the room for a moment before meeting her gaze. "Yes. Well, partly. I'm also looking for a job."

"A job?"

"I'm quitting the force. I can't seem to wrap my head around being part of a system that would release, and then protect, the likes of Ronaldo. His file has been sealed and the case closed. We've been told to stay away from him."

Ellen looked to Seline and he followed her gaze. Seline had her head cocked slightly to the side as though she were listening. She nodded then spoke. "Can we afford to keep him, Ellen?"

"Sure. We need another guy since Dan quit and moved out west. Okay, Detective Walsh, when can you start?"

"Two weeks. I'll spend as much time as possible during those two weeks snooping around, see if I can get a location for Ronaldo so Lady Shadow can question him."

Shadow was pacing now. She stopped beside his chair and gave his shoulder a gentle squeeze. "You said you have a name. What is it?"

"Linwood. The hot shot showed his ID and said his name was Special Agent Linwood. Ronaldo mentioned that name as a government contact in the drug trade before they showed up to spring him loose."

Lady Shadow grinned, showing her gleaming fangs. "Linwood. Oh yes, now I have a name and a face. Thank you, Detective Walsh, you've lived up to your end of the bargain. I have the scent once again."

"Victor, my name is Victor."

"Okay, Detective Victor Walsh," said Ellen, "before we go any farther with this, convince me this isn't a set up. Convince me you're not just undercover for the cops."

"He's not, Ellen."

"Can you be sure, Seline?"

"Moragah says we can trust him, and that we need him."

"Good enough for me," replied Ellen.

"Who is Moragah?"

"She's the goddess who made me what I am," replied Shadow. "Welcome to the bloodline."

"Okay, what does that mean?"

"Moragah is the Goddess of Wisdom and Defender of the Weak. I am one of only four priestesses she has created at this time. Our task is to defend the weak. In doing so, we gather a few people around us who have the courage and the heart to help us. They are utterly loyal to the priestess they serve. Moragah watches over them as best she can. They are called the bloodline. So, are you up for this? Will you serve the priestess of Moragah?"

He sat very still, absorbing the new information. "A goddess..." Shadow gripped his shoulder once again. Suddenly he was aware of that vast loving presence surrounding him, sweeping away all his fears and doubts. *Do not fear her, friend Victor Walsh. You know the rightness of her quest. She will need your help in the coming days, but that choice is yours to make. I will not compel you.*

"Oh my god, you're real."

He smiled as he felt the mirth in her reply. *"Oh yes, I'm quite real. So, will you serve me by aiding the priestess to stop the encroaching darkness?"*

"I will, I swear it."

"Welcome to the bloodline."

With that, Moragah withdrew from him, and he sighed to find himself alone in his body once again. "Holy smokes."

"That's Holy Moragah," smiled Ellen. "So?"

"I'm in, I swear it. What's our next move?"

Shadow patted his shoulder lightly. "As you said, you have two weeks yet with the police force. Learn what you can of Ronaldo and this Linwood. Ellen, do we still have John Daniels' cell phone in the safe? I think I should call our friend Linwood and see if I can rattle his cage a bit."

Two men sat in a room while three heavily armed men stood guard outside. It was Ronaldo and Linwood. "It's not that easy," complained Ronaldo. "That bitch has killed off most of my gang and nobody else wants to join. They have no courage."

"Unlike you," replied Linwood. "Some half baked cop grabs you and you sing like a bird. He roughs you up and you piss your pants, start babbling about a vampire riding a dragon. Good Christ man, grow a pair, for fuck's sake. There's a big shipment coming in day after tomorrow. You need to have your people in place and customers ready. We need that money. Do not screw this up."

"What about the cops?"

"I'll handle them. Don't worry about the cops. I ..." His cell phone rang and he thumbed it on. "Linwood, who the hell are you and how did you get that phone?"

"It's Daniels, you moron, and this is my phone, as issued by Uncle Sam's good government."

"You're dead."

"Yeah, right. Look, Linwood, we have to meet. This is way out of whack."

"So, you faked your death then went into hiding."

"Yes, and you'd better do the same and fast. Look, we have to meet. There are things you should know and things I need to know. I'll be down at the south side of the bridge. Meet me there in an hour. Linwood, come alone. Trust no one."

Linwood flicked off the phone and stared at it. "What the hell was that?" asked Ronaldo.

"Phone call from a dead man. Look, you know what you have to do. You don't have time to go raping and torturing women and children right now. Get your shit together and be at the docks day after tomorrow." With that he rose and left the building.

At the appointed time, Linwood pulled the car to a stop under the south side of the bridge. Slowly, a man appeared from the shadows and approached him. It was Daniels. "Sweet baby Jesus, it is you, John. How the hell did you pull that drowning thing off?"

"I had help. Now, listen to me. Jessica has disappeared."

"Reassigned, I know. Demoted, too, because you botched the clean up. Shit, John, this was an easy clean up. How the hell did it get so far out of hand?"

"I have no idea, but I do know this. That witness we tried to eliminate has some serious connections. She's still out there. Worse yet, she has a sister who's now in town looking for her. The sister is working for a P.I. named Cameron."

"I know. I plan to do something about that and soon."

"Don't. That's where it all goes sideways. Besides, they're small fish; they can't hurt us."

"So, what are you saying?"

"I'm saying we're the ones being cleaned, erased. Think about it. Who has the power and connections to take out so many of us all at once?"

Linwood's face was ashen. "Our bosses. Oh shit. Okay, what do we do, John? What's our move, or do we even have one?"

"There's only one way out of this and you know what that is."

"Find the threat and eliminate it. Jesus, you want to kill the top brass? How the hell do you expect to get away with that?"

"Doesn't matter now; I'm a marked man. They know I'm not dead and they're hunting for me. My only chance is to hit them first."

"So what about me? Where do I fit into all this?"

"Look, I've warned you what's going on. Get paranoid and stay that way. Trust no one."

"Okay. So, what do you want from me? I know you, John. You want something from me."

"I need to find Jessica Sacheck. She's the key. I find her and make her talk."

"Then follow the trail upwards until you find the kingpin. John, what if this goes all the way to the top?"

"I doubt that. Top brass has too much on their minds to pay attention to some little drug import op that has gone sideways. Somebody halfway up is covering their ass and that's who I have to find. So, where's Sacheck?"

"Riding a desk upstate for now, assigned to assist the FBI."

"What's her new name?"

"Caroline Winkle."

"For real?"

"For real."

Daniels laughed. "All right. She shouldn't be that hard to find. Watch your back, my friend." With that, he turned to walk away. Linwood fired several shots into his back. Daniels pitched forward and fell face down on the cold pavement. He twitched once, then lay still, blood pooling around his body.

"Stay dead this time," muttered Linwood, as he climbed back into his car and drove away.

Once Linwood's car disappeared around a building the body of John Daniels disappeared, dissolving into shadows. Another car came to life and slowly drove away. "Did you get the whole thing on video?" asked Ellen, as she turned the car towards home.

"Yep, got it all," replied Seline.

"Good. That'll make a fine ace in the hole if we need it."

The Lone Gunman

Victor Walsh went to work the next morning and gave his notice. When the captain asked him why, he told the truth. He was so sickened that a man like Ronaldo would be set free, he was leaving. When asked what he planned to do he said he was applying for a PI license. He could make a lot more money following cheating husbands and wives without the danger, and he wouldn't have to get near the likes of that slime Ronaldo ever again. The captain accepted, took his gun, and told him to ride a desk for the next two weeks. He didn't want any cowards out on the street.

Victor Walsh went home that night and took out a small electric device. He hit the button, and a high frequency squeal filled the room. There were two hisses and pops where two listening devices had been planted. Grinning, he retrieved a key from hiding, packed a small bag, and then went out again. A quick check of his car turned up no tracking devices, so he drove away.

An hour later he was at his parents' house. The old house was somewhat isolated just outside the city. His parents had moved to Europe six months past; the house was cold and empty feeling now.

He had always planned to move home. He guessed now was the time. He threw the overnight bag on the bed then went down to the basement. The old bookcase easily slid aside exposing the heavy door behind. He punched in the code and the door unlocked.

Inside was a well equipped arsenal. All his trophies for martial arts were on the shelf, too. He smiled wistfully for a moment, then selected two guns, extra ammunition, and a couple of throwing knives.

He tucked them away then locked up the hidden room, pushed the bookcase back into place, and returned to his apartment in town.

For the next two weeks he went to work, did his job, and then went home to watch TV. At least that's what the new listening devices told whoever was listening. While they listened to boring TV programs, he was busy in the darkened rooms. Training. He pushed hard to get his speed and form back in shape. For the life he was planning to lead, he would need to be in top form.

On his last day he turned in the badge and uniform, said goodbye to an eight year career, and walked away. The next day he packed up and left town. Victor Walsh had left the city. Later that night, after he had settled into the old house, he went to the garage and pulled the tarp off his father's muscle car. The jet black Viper roared to life and sped from the garage. An hour later, Ronaldo was gunned down by an unknown sniper.

Victor Walsh talked to himself as he sped homeward. "Well, Vic old boy, you've crossed the line now. A whole life dreaming of being the world's greatest detective gone to hell in a heartbeat."

"Yeah, well, it was never about being the great hero, it was about making a difference. With the system so totally fucked up, there was no other way. I'm hoping that goddess approves, because if she doesn't I'm screwed."

"Maybe we should ask her, but then, praying was never our strong suit. Ah hell, I'll just play this out as long as I can. With that scummy bastard off the streets, a lot of women can sleep easier. Lady Shadow will never know how badly I wanted to tear into that house with her. Actually, in hindsight, that's exactly what I should've done.

"All right, so now we're a vigilante. Can't be Batman, hate bats. Viper, that's who I'll be. I'll be the Viper, Lady Shadow's sidekick."

Further upstate Seline sat in a rental car, watching a rundown bar. She had located Jessica Sacheck and was now following her home. If she didn't come out soon, Seline was going to go in and get her.

Suddenly she felt the presence of Moragah grow stronger. She listened as Moragah told her about Victor Walsh and his transformation into the Viper.

"So he did go after Ronaldo after all."

"Yes. As long as he remained a policeman he played by their rules. However, as soon as he was free of the oath that restrained him, he acted."

"The Viper. I like it. Ah, there she comes. It's about time you came out of there, you drunken sot." Moragah chuckled and drew back to let Shadow work.

Jessica Sacheck went back to her small apartment. She stumbled once as she let herself in, then turned to lock the door. She felt the other presence in the room and pulled her gun. A cold dagger appeared at her throat then a colder voice spoke. "Drop it to the floor and step away." She obeyed. "Turn around."

As she turned, Jessica sobered up fast. There she was, the shadow woman the others had babbled about. "Who are you? What do you want? Are you going to kill me?"

"Perhaps," replied the apparition. She tossed her dagger into the air, and it became a staff. She caught the staff and used it to flick the gun across the room. "Sit down."

Jessica edged towards a chair then sat carefully. The shadow woman dropped the staff to the floor and it became a cobra, rising up and flaring it's hood while gazing intently at Jessica.

"Now then, Jessica Sacheck, or Caroline Winkle, or whatever your name truly is, we need to talk."

"Any name will do. What do I call you?"

"You may call me Shadow. Now, answer my questions truthfully and all will be well. Lie to me and he'll know." She indicated the snake. "His bite is fatal. Now then, you were the supervisor of a man named John Daniels, is that correct?"

"Yes."

"You sent him to kill Mrs. Alldon, did you not?"

"I don't know anything about ..." She got no further as the snake struck, sinking its deadly fangs into her arm and hanging on as she screamed and struggled. Shadow whistled and the snake released her, backing away. Horrified, Jessica looked at the puncture wounds on her arm.

As she looked up Shadow tossed her a vial. "The venom is swift. Already you can feel it burning in your veins, your breathing becoming more difficult. That is the antidote. Drink it all, every drop. It's equally as swift."

She waited until the woman had drained the vial then passed it back. Another moment longer and the woman's breathing returned to normal. "That was the last of the antidote. Do not test him again, for if you do I won't be able to help you."

"All right, yes, I ordered Daniels to clean up the mess that operation had become. He blew it. The witness is still in the wind, and I've been reassigned here to cover it all up. I told them it was a bad idea from the start. Once Brown made noises about blowing the whistle we should have folded our tents and moved on."

"But you were instructed to continue."

"Yes."

"By whom?"

"The supervisor for the region. His name is Terrance, Albert Terrance or it was when I was sent to this hell hole."

"Where would I find this man?"

"Back in the city. He has an office in a building owned by the company."

"By the company you mean the government. The CIA?"

She paused for a second, but the cobra flared its hood and she spoke. "Yes. The building is down near the docks. It is called the RH Import and Export Company. He has an office there. Look, that's all I can tell you. That's all I know. I ..." She suddenly realized she was alone. Lady Shadow and her pet cobra had vanished. Outside an old car pulled away from the curb and drove back towards the city.

Back on the Trail

Next morning, Seline arrived for work looking like she'd be happier going to bed. "Rough night?" asked Debbie. She and Victor had been having a cozy chat as Seline came through the door.

"Rough night," she replied. "Huh, looks like you two have been into the cuddle coffee already. Don't waste any time, do you, Debbie."

"Wasting time is for fools and losers," she replied, a bright smile on her face. "Right Vic, honey?"

He blushed deeply and shook a finger at her. "Woman, you're asking for it."

"I sure am. Does this mean I'm going to get some?"

"All right, you two are totally disgusting," said Seline. "Ellen in the office? Of course she is. No don't bother to announce me, I can find it by myself." They were smiling into each others eyes and ignoring her completely. She poured herself a coffee then tapped on the door to Ellen's office.

"Enter."

Seline stepped in and closed the door. "Hi there, did you miss me?"

Ellen rose and went to her, gently gathering the girl into her arms. "Yes, I missed you." She hugged Seline and spoke softly into her hair. "Next time call me or I swear, dragon or no dragon, I will bite you when you get home."

"Oh, now, you did miss me."

"Shut up and kiss me." Seline did as she was told, gently bringing her lips to Ellen's. The kiss was soft and warm, and yet it stirred her this time. She put a bit more enthusiasm into it and Ellen moaned with delight. Their lips parted and Ellen gazed into Seline's eyes. "Mmm, that had a bit more fire in it."

"Oh yeah, you taste good, woman. You know, I think that, with a bit of practice, we might get this kissing thing right."

At that point the door opened, and Debbie led Victor inside. "Okay, knock it off or get a room. This is a place of business." Debbie laughed and shrieked as Seline created a pillow and threw it at her. It vanished just before it struck.

"All right, people, settle down. Deb's right, we have to act mature so we don't scare away the clients." Ellen smiled as she kissed Seline's cheek then returned to her chair. "So, down to business. Detective Walsh, report."

"I got my P.I. license and I'm ready for actual cases. My last task: I followed the rich man's young bride and discovered her secret. She's volunteering at a homeless shelter and supporting it financially. She's not having an affair, nor is she paying blackmail. Here's the photos and a recording of my conversation with the shelter's manager."

"Good news. I'll deliver that report to the client this afternoon. Seline?"

"I found Jessica Sacheck or whatever the hell her name is now. Didn't have the heart to kill her and there was no reason. Her failure to eliminate me has put her well out of the action. She gave me the name of the next man up the ladder and a location. We're looking for Albert Terrance. He has an office in the building of the RH Import and Export Company."

"That's down by the docks," mused Victor.

"Yeah, she said it was. So, buddy of mine, tell us what you're not telling us."

"What? I have no idea..."

"Remember who you're talking to," said Seline, as she morphed into Lady Shadow. "You must not hold anything back from me, ever. Ellen and Debbie are my most trusted allies. You can speak freely with them. It's important to keep everybody in the loop at all times."

He sighed deeply and wouldn't meet her eyes. "All right, but now my life is in your hands, all of you. Two nights ago I moved back into my parents' house. There's a room there filled with weapons. My stepdad also left the keys to his baby, a jet black Viper. I loaded up a sniper rifle, took the Viper and came back to the city. Ronaldo has raped his last victim. I killed the bastard and I'm not one damn bit sorry."

"Nor am I," said Shadow. "Now the rest of it."

He was blushing now, and Debbie's eyes opened wide as he spoke. "I can't, it's too embarrassing."

"Hey, none of that, mister. Out with it," said Debbie.

He blushed even deeper. "I sent the police a message. Said I was the new game in town and all criminals should beware. I called myself the Viper. I know, foolish, and childish."

"I don't know," grinned Debbie. "I kinda like it."

"As do I," said Shadow. "Stand up."

Puzzled, he rose to his feet. She smiled at him for a moment then waved her hand in the air. He felt a tingle then caught a glimpse of himself in the wall mirror. He was dressed in black leather from head to toe, a picture of a viper on the chest of his armor, and a hood that had a snake's face on it. He could feel the weight of the leather and hear it creak softly as he moved, testing its flexibility.

"Like it, Viper?"

"This is awesome." He had daggers sheathed in his boots, more knives up his sleeves, guns at the hips and one inside the vest beneath his arm.

"I foresee a time when we'll have use of this disguise," said Shadow, as she returned to Seline form and he returned to T-Shirt and jeans. "You are now Victor Walsh, code name, Viper."

"Cool. So, what are we up to today?"

"You can locate Mr. Terrance while Seline goes home and gets some sleep," said Ellen. "Debbie, see what you can find out about that Import Export company."

Ellen arrived home to find Shadow in a chair, reading. A number of small woodland creatures were gathered around and Aeroth was guarding the door. The dragon gave her a friendly nudge as she hung up her coat. She gave him a rub under the chin then poured up a glass of wine and joined Shadow in the living room. "So, did you get any rest at all?"

"I meant to, but I wanted to read another chapter, and, well, you know how it is."

"One chapter led to another?"

"Yeah, pretty much. How was your day?"

"Pretty good, actually. I do enjoy giving clients good news. We earned a fat bonus from two different cases. Also, Debbie says the Import Export business is a front for the CIA, and Victor spent the day watching them, but nobody came or went. He said it almost looked abandoned."

"Okay, so I blew it leaving Sacheck alive. Obviously she's alerted them."

"Maybe, maybe not. Give it a couple of days. See what happens."

"Yeah, I guess you're right. Maybe I'll go with Vic tomorrow. I can tune in, maybe hear or see something inside."

"About Victor, what do you plan to do with him?"

"Do with him?"

"He's really got a hard on for cleaning out the gangs. I'm afraid he'll go on a spree and get you killed trying to protect him."

"Ellen, are you worried about me?"

"So, what if I am?"

"I think that's so sweet."

"Yeah, well, he's taking Debbie out, too, and I don't want her to get hurt either."

"Okay, I'll reign him in and see what I can do to help him at the same time. After what those guys did, I have to say I'm on his side with the cleaning out the gangs thing. Ellen, I also understand that we can't afford to have the authorities figure out we're behind Lady Shadow and the Viper, either. We need to tighten it up."

"Thanks, sweetie. I know we have to do this, but we're planning to play hardball with some very powerful people. If they come at us full force there is no way in hell we can survive. We have to stay under their radar."

"Point taken. This is why I came to you in the first place. I do need your skills and guidance, so don't ever hesitate to speak up."

"So you still need me, even though you have a new sidekick."

Seline rose to her feet and crossed to the sofa to sit beside Ellen. She gently pulled the woman into her arms. "Whoa there, sweet lady. Where did that come from?"

"Sorry, I..."

"Hush now, Shadow's got you." Ellen could suddenly feel the leather of her armor. "I'll work with Viper, make sure he's on side and fully aware of the dangers. And, pay close attention now, and every night I will come home to you. Ellen, that kiss this morning held a lot of promise and I want to explore that with you."

"Seline, I'm so sorry. I've never felt like this before, not for anyone. I guess I'm not handling it very well."

Shadow morphed back into Seline. "Hush now, you need to eat and so do I. After that we will explore the kissing thing again. Okay?"

"Let me get this straight, if I eat all my dinner I get dessert?"

"Oh yeah, baby."

"Come on then, kitchen's this way." She took Seline by the hand and dragged her towards the kitchen.

Seline smiled and listened to Ellen sing to herself while she cooked. When the meal was finished Ellen gazed at Seline and sighed. "Seline, what are we going to do?"

"You mean about us or the extended family business?"

"Oh, I think the *us* will have lots of fun working itself out. I mean the rest of it. Do you honestly believe we can survive?"

"Oh yes, survive and thrive, but as I said, you're right. We need to tighten up, first Viper and I, and then all four of us. I'll confer with Moragah before we do anything else drastic. Tomorrow I just want to confirm that the export company is where I locate Terrance. We won't approach him until both you and I are satisfied the clan is safe and ready."

"Thank you. I was starting to worry that..."

"We'd never get to practice the kissing thing?"

Ellen grinned. "Yeah, that. Oh look, we seem to have a bit of spare time right now. Should we practice?"

"Absolutely. How about on a beach under a full moon?"

"How about right here on the couch?"

"That works too. Take me away."

"With extreme pleasure." Ellen took Seline's hand and led her to the sofa. She turned down all the lights then settled down beside her. She gently pulled Seline to her and kissed her softly. Seline moaned with delight and avidly returned the kiss. When their lips parted Ellen began kissing along Seline's jawline, nipping gently at the spots that elicited a gasp. She worked her way down the girl's throat to the edge of her cleavage. She returned to capture Seline's mouth with her own, hungry for her, devouring her.

Seline moaned with delight then gasped as delicate fingers found their way into her bra and pinched her nipple to life. "Ellen, what are you doing to me?"

"Seducing you, silly woman."

"Thank god for that," replied Seline. She surged to her feet, scooping Ellen into her arms.

"Seline, what are you doing?"

"Carrying you upstairs to the bedroom where you can do a proper job of that seduction."

"Damn fine idea," murmured Ellen, as she nestled her head on Seline shoulder. "Hurry it up, I want to get back to what I was doing." Seline laughed with delight as she jogged up the stairs with the woman in her arms.

Dawn found them still asleep, the bed in a shambles. Ellen was the first to wake. She smiled with pure delight to find Lady Shadow cuddled in her arms. She softly kissed the girl's hair and snuggled her closer.

Mid-morning found Seline and Victor sipping coffee and watching a building down by the docks. It was the import/export building. "I still don't see any signs of life," grumbled Vic.

"There's a few cars in the parking lot," mused Seline, as she passed the binoculars over to him. "Let me see if I can find any life inside." She closed her eyes and began to breathe deeply. A short while later she opened them again and sighed. "Yeah, he's in there and so is Linwood. I'm going to see if I can listen in. Can you take the car a little closer?"

"We could get spotted."

"Yeah, maybe you're right. Okay, this is a bit far away, but I'll give it a shot." She closed her eyes once again and began to focus. It took a moment, then she was able to faintly hear the two men in the office.

"That's about it, sir," said Linwood. "The product is now in circulation and the profits are coming in. This was a big shipment, and it took a while to find enough distributors, but it's moving now and the funds are starting to pile up."

"That's good to know. Took you long enough to get those distributors in place. I thought you people had everything under control."

"We did, but that sick bastard Ronaldo fucked everything up with that gang initiation of his."

"What does that have to do with it? I agree he's a sick fuck, but a truly effective distributor. You know the rules, we don't mess with the distributor's business."

"It wasn't our people. Somehow, someone with a lot of firepower and money got involved. They made up a story about some alien woman doing the killing and they cleaned out Ronaldo's entire organization. We managed to spring him, but another vigilante showed up and popped him off. Worse yet, half my team has been killed trying to clean up that mess about the whistle blower."

"Speaking of that, where do we stand with it?"

"It was a complete mess, but I believe we have it controlled."

"What aren't you telling me?"

"Daniels faked his own death; I don't know how he managed it. He contacted me a few days ago. We met, he warned me someone higher up was gunning for us, then started to pump me for information."

"What did you do?"

"I shot the bastard."

"You're certain he's dead this time?"

"Oh yeah. I emptied a clip into him and watched to make sure he was gone."

The other man sighed deeply and sank back into his chair. "Dammit, this is a complete screw up from start to finish, the body count is piling up, and we're in danger of being exposed if we don't get control."

"We have it, sir. All the loose ends have been tied up."

"Including Sacheck?"

"It's done, Sir. We're completely in the clear. The shipment has arrived and is being distributed. The police will have their hands full with the drug problem now. They'll have to put the killings on the back burner. The money is rolling in. Mission going according to plan."

"Jesus I hate doing things this way. If those damn fools in Congress would just fund us properly we wouldn't have to do things like this."

"Yeah, I will admit, when I signed on I didn't expect to be working on home soil like this."

"It's all a game, Linwood, a fools game. We operate outside the country to keep the country safe but, to do that, we have to destroy lives within, here at home. A small pain for a much greater gain. That's how we have to look at it. Yes, we destroy some lives here, but we save so many more by keeping our enemies at bay elsewhere. The worst part is, we dare not let the general public know or the whole house of cards will fall."

"Yeah, I get that. That's the real problem, most people can't see the bigger picture."

Seline sighed and opened her eyes. "Good Christ, these guys really believe they're the good guys."

"But we're the real good guys?"

"Vic, we need to go someplace safe to have a long talk. Someplace private."

"Shadow?"

"Trust me."

"All right, it's about an hour's drive, but we can go to my place outside the city. We can pick up a pizza on the way."

"Works for me." She settled back in the car as he drove. He didn't try to engage her in conversation. He had a feeling something big was up. He left her to her own thoughts.

Although it looked like Seline was just being introspective, she wasn't. She was talking to Moragah, discussing her plan, and asking for help. "Lady Moragah?"

"I am here, my priestess."

"I need your advice; I need your help."

"State your need, my child."

"I need to convince this big lug to keep a low profile. I need to find a way to keep him safe. I also need to keep Ellen and Debbie safe.

Vic has to understand how important it is to stay off the government's radar."

"Yes, I do agree with your assessment. Do you have a plan?"

"The girls know we have to stay low. It's Vic that I need to convince. I think he may have a Batman complex."

"I think he is more aware than he lets show. He makes light of things so people cannot see the depth of his true feelings. I believe he will listen to you. If all else fails I will speak with him."

"Thanks, Lady Moragah. Now about the keeping him safe thing. I have an idea, but I'm not so sure I can do it or if you would approve."

"Tell me what you have in mind."

"Did you see when I put him in armor yesterday?"

"I did."

"I know I can make that armor real, but I want to teach him how to call the armor even if I'm not there. Call it and make it real, like a part of him."

"I cannot make him a priestess, Seline. He is male. It doesn't work with them."

"That sounds like you've tried before."

"I have. Each time I did, the male eventually became obsessed with power, and I had to destroy him."

"Understood and accepted. Lady, I don't ask for super powers for him, just some armor to help him stay alive." Seline swallowed hard. She felt Moragah's hesitation and was afraid she had crossed a line that should never be crossed. "Lady, if you don't approve, then I'll find another way."

Moragah enveloped Seline in that warm loving embrace again and the girl relaxed completely. *"Be at peace, my priestess. We will do this, but he needs to know the risks."*

"I'll make sure he does." With that Moragah withdrew.

Seline opened her eyes and gazed around. They were driving along a country road lined with trees. It was peaceful. Victor turned down a long driveway towards a small house nestled against the edge of the forest. "Come in, let's demolish that pizza and you can tell me what's up."

They finished the pizza, but Victor was having trouble getting Seline to talk. He showed her around the house. She admired the weapons room, but still seemed to be lost in thought. When he showed her the training room where he'd trained for martial arts all his young life, his day got weird quickly. She grabbed him and threw him against the wall, hard.

Victor grunted with the impact and started to fall, but caught himself against the wall. "What the fuck?"

"Defend yourself." She came at him then. He fought with all his skills but found himself losing. She caught him and threw him against the wall again. "Stop holding back. Fight me or I'll put you down."

He came at her, but she was too strong and way too fast. He was soon backed into a corner, even though he had tried a lot harder. Suddenly she stopped and stepped back. "Was that your best?"

"Yes, what the hell is going on?"

"You need to train. Here's what's going on. You haven't felt even half my strength nor have you seen half my speed. What did you learn?"

"That I'm not in your league."

"Good. Lesson one out of the way. If we're in a fight together, never try to defend or protect the poor little girl. That would be an instinct with you, to protect the weak, the girl."

"Yeah, it would."

"And normally it would be a good one, just not with me, ever. If I need you, I'll ask."

"Okay, got it."

"Next lesson." She waved her arm, and he was suddenly back in the armor, complete with bladed weapons. "Defend yourself."

She leaped at him and he fought back. The leather was heavy and restrictive, but it did protect him. She hurled him against the wall. "Use the weapons."

"Seline..."

"Do it!"

He drew the daggers. He'd practiced with such weapons in class, but only with forms. However, the forms were helping. Having to avoid the blades kept her at bay more and she had a harder time getting past his guard. Soon he was holding his own. "Now you're holding back."

"Yes, but not as much as you think." She stepped back and stopped. "So, armor or no armor?"

"Armor for sure, but it won't be a lot of use against a bullet."

"Armor piercing, no, but standard loads, yes. The hardened leather will slow them down and the silk underneath will stop them. Are you comfortable in the armor."

"Yes, but you're holding back. Don't." She nodded then came in again. Just as she reached him she blurred out of sight, his weapons were battered aside and he was hurled against the wall with enough force to drive the air from his lungs." She came back into view, breathing deeply, and offered him a hand up. He accepted and was easily hauled to his feet.

What's this all about?"

"It's about the Viper. I don't know if you'd thought it through when you pulled that stunt and claimed to be the new Batman, but you can't undo it now. I also can't be with you day and night to bring up the armor. You need to learn how to do it for yourself."

"Fair enough, but why kick the stuffings out of me?"

"Experience is the best teacher. I could tell you a hundred times that I didn't need protecting, but you'd still try to do it."

"And you'd end up trying to protect me when I got in too deep then we'd both get killed. Got it."

"Come here," she said as she sat and patted the bench beside her. "Vic, the world's different now. We were both brought up to learn our place in the world, you to be a protector and me to be a nurturer, am I right?"

"That's true all right. That's why I wanted to be a cop, to protect and serve. To defend the weak from the bad guys."

"And I was brought up to be a good little girl and do what I was told, to serve the men and fear God. That's changed for both of us now for lots of reasons. First of all, there's no real way to tell the good guys from the bad guys now."

"I thought we're supposed to be the good guys."

"We are, by our standards, but so are the people I'm after. They believe themselves to be the good guys too, just doing what's necessary for the greater good. Vic, we're not the good guys, the bad guys, nor are we super heroes. We're Lady Shadow and the Viper."

"Something very different from both of the standard concepts. Okay, so where does that leave us?"

"We serve Moragah, in any way She wants. The laws of men don't matter, and our upbringing doesn't matter. Just as I can't run and hide when a man gets angry or hold back when I fight a youngster like those kids trying to join that gang, you can't go jumping in..."

"Gotcha, but aren't we supposed to defend the weak?"

"Yes, we are, but try this: you see two big cops beating the crap out of a known pedophile. He's obviously weaker. What do you do?"

"I see your point. If I stop the cops the scumbag gets away, but if I ignore it... What should I do in that situation?"

"That will be your call to make, my friend. I just wanted to point out it isn't always cut and dried. Another thing, and this is the most important to hammer home. You need to keep the Viper anonymous. Vic, the people we're up against are powerful, highly placed, and they firmly believe they're in the right, they're the good guys. Vic, if they even get a whiff of who we truly are they'll come at us heavy. The first two casualties will be..."

"Ms Cameron and Debbie. Seline..."

"First up; between us, Vic, there can be no bullshit, no secrets, no bravado, and no games. Agreed?"

He nodded his head slowly. "Agreed. I understand what you're saying, and I agree. No games and no secrets. So how do we do what we have to do and still protect them?"

"The Viper can do what he has to do, but Victor Walsh can't. When we're at work or whatever, you can never let your true power show. Victor Walsh needs to be a bit of a scaredycat. Seline Elmore, too."

"But the girls will know, right? I mean, they know about you, but ..."

"You don't want your girlfriend thinking you're a pussy, right?"

"Busted. This isn't going to be easy."

"Relax, Debbie's in the loop and I want her to stay there. She knows who you are. I ask you now, think hard, if you can't live this, keep the secret, live the lie, then back away now. Once I teach you to call the armor there's no going back."

He did as she bid him, giving it a long moment's thought. "Seline, what happens if I get the armor and then go off script?"

"That must never be allowed to happen, Vic."

"But if it does?"

"Moragah will send me after you."

"And that's another reason you kicked the crap out of me, to dispel any illusions I might entertain once I get a taste of the power. All right, Shadow. I'm in. Teach me how to call the armor."

They began and by the time darkness fell he could get it two out of three times. They gave it up for the day and he drove her back to town. Ellen and Debbie were still waiting at the office when they arrived. Seline gave a full report then they called it a day. A week later Vic could bring the armor and weapons in a heartbeat, armor, daggers, guns, and snake mask. The Viper was ready for action.

Captured

Monday morning, after a gentle weekend spent at Vic's country home, they all sat in Ellen's office watching the morning news on the TV. While they'd taken long gentle walks in the woods and enjoyed evening barbecues, the city had gone to hell. There had been a shootout between two rival gangs over drugs and territory. New people were moving into Ronaldo's old territory and the war was on.

A lot of innocent people had been caught in the crossfire. Several were killed and many more wounded. The police were making a lot of noise in the media, but not much else. The mayor and state governor both were making speeches and promising a task force. Vic just shook his head. "That's exactly what's needed here," he grumbled, "a task force to study the problem."

Ellen sighed deeply. She'd hit the pause button, and the picture froze on the face of a young girl whose face had been nearly shot off. She was wrapped in bandages with just her eyes showing. Those eyes looked terrified.

"Oh my dear sweet lord," said Debbie. "That poor child."

Ellen saw as Seline morphed into Shadow and Viper put on his armor. "Stop that, both of you. Not here, not now." Viper looked like he might argue, but Shadow returned to Seline. "Yes, dear. So, are we just going to ignore this?"

Vic lost the armor and sat back down. "This isn't our battle, is it?" asked Ellen.

"I think it is," replied Seline. "Look how many innocents got caught up in that mess. Look who got hurt, children, women, old people..."

"All right, sweetheart, but we have to be careful here. Vic, get an old picture from the files, then head down to the police station. Tell them you're looking for someone who might have been caught in the gun battle. See what you can find out about who was shooting at who, why, and where to find them. Debbie, you work the same thing from here. Seline and I will hit the street and see if we can learn anything."

Ellen and Seline sat sipping their coffee. The cafe was busy, and the topic of the day was the shootings. Seeming to be lost in their own thoughts, they nonetheless managed to hear a great deal.

"I don't know, but I do know this, it's all that Shadow woman's fault. That man Ronaldo had the streets under control, he kept the junkies out of sight and didn't bother decent people."

"Yeah, well I heard it was a new guy, the Viper, who plugged Ronaldo."

"Doesn't matter. Whoever it was threw the who city wide open for a gang war. They'll kill half of us before another strong man takes over and settles things down."

Disgusted, Seline started to rise, but Ellen kicked her under the table then shook her head. Seline went back to listening.

"... don't understand why the police can't seem to do anything about all this. I mean, Jesus. What do we pay taxes for?"

"The whole country is out of control. I'm on my way to buy a gun. I'm tired of taking chances."

"My husband says it's really the government doing this. He says ..."

It went on and on. They heard things that were sickening and frightening. However, at the bottom of it all, they learned nothing useful. They left and went to another coffee shop. Sadly, it was just more of the same. It was late in the afternoon when they finally caught a break.

They were driving slowly through the seedier part of town, Ellen behind the wheel and Seline listening with her extended hearing.

Suddenly she reached out and patted Ellen's arm. Ellen pulled over to the curb and pretended to be making a phone call.

"I tell you Ricky, I saw what I saw. It was the fed Ronaldo used to work with."

"Driving the car?"

"Yeah, driving the car. Look, I think that fed is who started the shootout."

"Why the hell would he do that. They bring in the drugs, we sell them. Why would they shoot the shit out of us?"

"Bait. I think that bastard used us as bait."

"What the hell are you talking about?"

"Look, they say it was that Shadow woman who cleaned out the old gang. Viper popped Ronaldo. I think the fed used the turf war to draw them out."

"Oh, for fuck's sake."

"No, think about it. When was the last time those guys came into our territory shooting?"

"Never."

"So why now and why is a fed driving for them?"

"Okay, say you're right about this, what do we do? We need those drugs to operate. That means we can't pop the fed."

"No, but we can scare the shit out of him though. Make him understand we don't appreciate our turf getting all shot up for no reason."

"Yeah, well, you work on that plan. I've got shit to do."

That conversation was over, and Seline sighed as she related it to Ellen. "Actually, I think our unknown friend may just be right about this," said Ellen as she pulled out into traffic again. "Let's go back to the office and check in with the others."

They arrived back at the office to find Debbie and Vic snuggled up by her computer. "Well, this looks cozy," remarked Seline, a grin of pure mischief on her face.

"Shadow, come here," said Vic, not looking up from the screen. "You gotta see this."

Ellen and Seline peered over Debbie's shoulder. "This is financial records," said Ellen. "Who are we looking at here?"

"Agent Linwood," grinned Vic.

"Wow," said Seline, "my buddy Linwood has done quite well for himself."

"It seems so. I heard his name a few times at the police station today. Seems Agent Linwood has pulled rank on the locals and is conducting the investigation himself."

"Yeah, and he was driving one of the shooters' cars as well," said Seline. "I'm starting to think our man Linwood might just be at the root of a lot of problems in this city. I also wonder if Agent Terrance is aware of this or is he involved?"

"I checked his financials, didn't look like he was holding anything back."

Seline sighed and straightened up. "I believe you, Debbie. From what little I've learned about Agent Terrance, he wouldn't do that. He sees himself as one of the good guys. Linwood is just a back shooting son of a bitch. Vic, you need a hiding place here in town for that super car of yours."

"I do? Why?"

"Because I don't want to walk all the way back home from the docks tonight, and if I'm seen crawling into a car then I want it to be the Viper."

"So, we're going after Linwood tonight?"

"No, I want a chat with Terrance first."

"Okay, I know where I can hide it. I'll be back in a couple of hours."

As Vic left to fetch the Vipermobile, as he called it, Seline turned back to Debbie. "You covered your tracks, right? These guys can't track this back to you?"

"Nope, we're clear."

"Good. Have you found an address for Terrance?"

"Yes, but it turns out to be a dud."

"I'll track him home," said Ellen. "Seline, keep your phone handy. Wait here until Vic gets back. I should have an address for you by then."

"I should come with you."

"I've got this, Honey. You catch some rest while you can." With that she was out the door.

"Well, crap," muttered Seline. "Deb, if anybody wants me I'll be napping on the couch in Ellen's office."

"Yes, ma'am," grinned Debbie, as she returned her attention to the computer screen.

Two hours later, Victor found her pacing in the outer office. "Ellen not back yet?"

"No, nor is there any word from her. I..."

"Hi, kids, sorry I'm late," grinned Ellen, as she stepped through the door. "The guy's a real keener; he worked late. Here's his address."

Seline inspected the slip of paper Ellen gave her then nodded and passed it to Victor. "You're amazing," she said as she kissed Ellen's cheek. "I'll be home as soon as I can."

"Don't go after Linwood until we've all had a chance to debrief and make a plan."

"Yes, dear. Come on, Vic. Let's go play at Terrance's house." Grinning, he followed her out.

Ellen and Debbie watched them go. "Chinese this time?" inquired Ellen.

"Oh yeah, I'm starved." They closed up the office then went to their favorite Chinese restaurant.

Vic put Seline in his old car and drove away. He soon turned towards the warehouse district. Approaching an old building he pulled out a remote and hit the button. A large door opened up and he drove in. As the door closed again the lights came on. The building was little more than a closed in alley with a door at both ends. There was the shiny black Viper ready to go. They changed to the super car then headed out again.

Viper drove right into the driveway of the private residence. Seline had already morphed into Shadow and Vic donned his armor as Shadow opened the locked door. They stepped inside and a woman screamed. Terrance faced them, gun in hand and a woman hiding behind him. "You picked the wrong house to invade, scumbags," he growled.

Moving too fast for him to react to, Shadow leaped at him and stripped away the gun. She tossed him through the air to land heavily on the couch. The woman tried to flee, but Viper blocked her path. He silently pointed to the couch, and she went to sit beside Terrance. Shadow reached out and touched the woman's shoulder. She fainted.

"Is this woman your wife?"

"Yes. Please don't hurt her. Take whatever you want and ..."

"We're not here to rob you. She'll sleep until we leave then you can tell her she dreamed our visit."

"Okay, if you're not robbers then who are you?"

"You know who we are," she replied. "I'm Lady Shadow; he's Viper. We're here to exchange information and to deliver an ultimatum."

"What ultimatum?"

"Information first. You are an agent of the CIA, are you not?"

"No. Whatever made you think ...?"

He got no further as she snapped her fingers and a staff with a carved snake's head appeared in her hand. She dropped it to the floor and it became a cobra which reared up and flared its hood, staring into his eyes. "This is Minx, he can tell if you lie to me, and if you do, he will strike. His venom is swift and fatal. Do not test me again. So, you are CIA, yes?"

He swallowed hard, his eyes fixed on the snake. "Yes."

"You are Agent Linwood's supervisor, are you not?"

"Yes."

"Are you aware that Linwood is the man who caused the gun battle in the city this weekend past?"

"No, what makes you think that?"

"He was seen driving one of the shooter's cars."

"No way, that's not possible."

"Why not?"

"Well, he wouldn't do that. I mean, what reason would he have?"

"Did you order him to do this?"

"What??? No."

She glanced at the snake, but it didn't waver. She nodded as she absorbed the information. "Very well. Let us try another line of inquiry. Did you order the executions of Mr. and Mrs. Brown?"

"They weren't married." The snake moved closer. "Yes, yes, I ordered Brown silenced. She was collateral damage."

"There seems to be a lot of that in your world."

"I know. Look, I know what you must think, but we do what we have to do to stop the enemies of this country before they reach our soil. It sucks, but it is what it is."

"You truly believe in this, sacrificing your own people to this cause?"

"I don't like it, but yes, it has to be done."

"That's what the priests used to say as they sacrificed people to the gods to bring rain thousands of years ago. It was false then and it's false now. I give you one chance and one chance only. Cease importing drugs and I'll let you live."

"Fine, I can do that, and I'll be killed or shipped out the north pole, another man will take my place."

"The orders will come from above?"

"You know they will."

"Who? Who will give that order? The director?"

"Oh no, he will retain plausible deniability. Someone close to him will give the order and take the fall if necessary."

His answer seemed to anger her, and the snake became agitated. Viper stepped forward to lay a hand on her shoulder for a moment then he stepped back. She was calm again. She began pacing. "Very well, let it be what it must, but my offer of a single chance stands. Find another way. Tell those above you the same. I'll follow the trail all the way to the top if I must, and I'll destroy all in my path to do so.

"Now, information for you. Are you aware that Agent Linwood has become extremely wealthy from the drug trade? Also, he has taken the case of the weekend's shooting out of the hands of the local police. They have been warned to stay away from the gangs. Have you commanded any of this?"

"What? No, I didn't. Look, we had nothing to do with that gang shootout. We have no reason to interfere. Linwood is skimming? The bastard. I'll put a stop to that."

"Then our business here is complete. Come, Viper, we have places to go, people to see." She swept up the cobra, which became a staff once again. She touched Terrance with it and he, too, fainted. They left and roared away in the Viper. Two blocks away they stopped and waited. It wasn't long before Terrance left the house. They followed. He returned to the office where Linwood was waiting for him. Vic parked the car closer this time to make it easier for Shadow to hear what was going on inside.

"Hey boss, What's up?" asked Linwood as Terrance stormed into the office.

"You are, Linwood. Shit, I can understand the skimming, but running with the gangs during a shootout? What the hell were you thinking?"

"So, you finally got wise. What was I thinking? I was thinking territory. That asswipe Ronaldo was fine to use as a front, but he was a truly sick bastard, and I was happy when the Viper popped him. However, that left a hole in the local power structure. I decided to take over, cut out the middle man, and increase the profits."

"You traitorous son of a bitch, Linwood."

"Oh don't give me that old "saving American lives" bullshit. You and I both know those crazy bastards out in the deserts are no real threat. This was always about protecting the oil profits for the super rich guys. Why the hell shouldn't I get a piece of the action?"

"She's going to kill you, you know. That Shadow woman. She'll put you down and I'll cheer her on. You're finished, Linwood."

"Oh, for fuck's sake." There was the sound of gun shots, then silence for a moment before Linwood spoke again. "Yeah, sorry to wake you. Terrance got wise. I think that Lady Shadow woman ratted me out. What do you want to do? Already done. Yes, he's dead. I'll dispose of the body. Look, I don't have his overseas connections, but I can handle distribution. Just get the stuff here and I'll handle the rest. Okay, two. Just send me two agents you can trust. Yes, sir. Consider it done."

Shadow sighed and broke her connection to them. "Linwood killed Terrance. He then called someone, probably Terrance's supervisor. He's been given this territory and will have new agents with him soon. This whole thing sickens me, Viper."

"So, what do you want to do?"

"Go home. Let's call it a night, then get Ellen's take on it in the morning."

"That makes sense," he replied, as the big car roared to life and sped away. "That girl is smarter than any ten people I know rolled together. She'll know what to do."

"I sure hope so," sighed Shadow, "for I'm all at sea here. Cripes, is no one in government service trustworthy? Do none of them trust any of the others? Are they all plotting against each other as well as the people they're supposed to serve?"

He made no reply, just left her to her thoughts. They traded cars again, shifted back into Vic and Seline, then he drove her home.

Ellen was waiting up, reading in the library. She rose and came to meet Seline as she heard the door. It wasn't Seline. Two men wearing masks and holding guns grabbed her and pulled a bag over her head. She struggled as she felt the prick of the syringe. A moment later her world went fuzzy, and her struggles ceased.

Seline should have waited longer. Had she done so she would have overheard Linwood giving instructions to the kidnappers. As it was, she arrived home to find the door ajar, the lock broken, and the place empty. A glance told her Ellen's keys were in the tray so she should have been home. She called out, then ran from room to room but found nothing. She whipped out her phone and called Victor.

"Seline? Calm down girl. What's happened?"

"The place was broken into, and Ellen is missing."

"Fuck. On my way back."

"No, Vic. Get to Debbie and take her to a place of safety. I'll find Ellen and there'll be hell to pay." She shut off the phone and morphed into Shadow. "Aeroth!" The dragon slipped from the shadows. "Ellen has been taken. Find her. Find Ellen." The beast snuffled about for a minute then went through the door. She followed, closing it behind her. He went to the elevator then turned to look at her. She nodded and he vanished. She rode down to the underground parking area.

Stepping out of the elevator, she gestured, and the dragon reappeared from the shadows. He caught the scent, then followed it to a parking stall where he stood snuffling for a moment then turned and headed for the exit. He lost the scent in the mix of automobile vapors on the street. "No matter, my darling; I think I know who has her." With that, Shadow swung easily to his back then the dragon leaped to the sky.

She guided him towards the docks to land atop the import/export building. Leaning against the mighty beast's shoulder, Shadow searched the building with her extra sight. Ellen was not there, but Linwood was. He sat behind his former boss's desk, a grin on his face. There were blood stains on the floor but no body in evidence. She was about to go after him when he answered his phone.

"Yeah?"

"She's coming around, boss. What should we do? Should we pop her?"

"No, you idiot, we need her alive. As long as we have her we can control that Shadow woman. Just keep her quiet and wait for further instructions." He hummed to himself for a moment then laughed out loud. "Come on, Shadow, you slut. You know I've got your girl. Come to me. Come on, come threaten me. Show me your bag of tricks. Oh yeah, you're going to make me far richer than I ever dreamed possible."

"Not in this lifetime, moron," she muttered. "All right, Shadow, think girl, think. Where would they take her? Who does he trust to do this? The gangsters. We need Viper." She took out her phone and called.

"Walsh."

"Viper, is all well?"

"I have Debbie and she's unhurt. Where ..."

"I'll meet you at the Vipermobile's home." She dropped the phone back into her pocket then mounted the dragon's back again. Vic was just arriving with Debbie as the dragon dropped from the sky to land beside the door. She hugged the beast then he vanished into the shadows. The big door rose, Vic drove inside, and Shadow followed. Once the door closed, She brought them up to speed.

"What should we do?" asked Debbie. She was clearly upset and frightened.

"Are you able to drive?" asked Shadow.

"What? Yes, I can drive."

"Go to Vic's country house. We'll retrieve Ellen then meet you there."

Debbie swallowed hard then nodded. Vic passed her the keys then raised the big door for her to back out. Once she was on the way he lowered the door again and turned to Shadow, his armor appearing as he moved. "Okay, do we know where they're hiding her?"

"No, but I thought you might know where the gangs hang out, where they might be."

"I know of a few places they might be. Why aren't we beating it out of Linwood?"

"Because he wants to control me. He's expecting me to come at him. He's too confident. Something is amiss and I don't like it. They won't harm her unless he gives the word, so we find her while he waits for me to appear. Dammit, how did he know Ellen and I are close anyway?"

"He's probably had people watching you. I worked out who you are; I'm sure he could too. We need a new plan."

"That's my lady's job and she can get to it just as soon as we find her and bring her home. You drive. Let's go bust up some gangsters."

"All my pleasure, Lady Shadow." The door raised, the big car roared to life and sped out into the city. "There's one thing you need to understand, Shadow."

"Once we ask the question they will all know, and Ellen will be in mortal danger."

"Yes. You know what that means."

"I do. None of them may remain alive. I have no problems with that. I tire of this. It's now time to clean up this city."

"Okay, we're here," said Viper, as he pulled up near a house in the poor section of town.

"Let's go." Together they strode up to the door then Seline kicked it down. She was inside like a whirlwind and people fell, guns clattered to the floor and amid the carnage stood the Viper, an automatic weapon in each hand. Those Shadow had thrown to the floor shrank in fear of the masked warrior who held the weapons.

Shadow reappeared, dragging two more young men by the collars. She dumped them on the floor at Viper's feet. "I have questions," she said, her voice cold as deep space.

"What the fuck do you want?" demanded one of the men.

He screamed as Viper shot him in the foot. "She asks the questions. You provide the answers. Any deviation from this path will have painful consequences." The man nursed his wounded foot and nodded.

"This night a woman was kidnapped on the orders of Agent Linwood. Where is she?"

"I don't know what..." The others recoiled in horror as Viper shot him through the chest. Shadow stepped to the next one. "This night a woman was kidnapped from her home at the request of Agent Linwood. Where is she?"

"Look, I don't know anything, I mean, yes, we know Linwood, but we don't know anything about no kidnapping."

It was just a flicker of movement, but Shadow caught it. A girl screamed as a snake latched onto her hand and her phone fell to the floor. "His venom is swift and fatal," she said, as she turned and retrieved the phone. There was a voice on the other end. The girl's eyes rolled back in her head, and she fell sideways to the floor and lay still.

"Gina, Gina, what the hell is going on? Answer me."

"Gina is dead," said Shadow, as she spoke into the phone. "As will you be soon. I am Shadow. You have someone who is quite dear to me; I want her back unharmed. If I find her that way you might survive. If she has been harmed I will rain down destruction on you in a way you could not imagine." The phone went dead, and she cast it aside.

Viper grabbed one man by the shirt and hauled him to his feet. He slammed the man against the wall. "Where is she?"

"Fuck you."

"Shadow, may I borrow the cobra?"

Shadow materialized the staff and tossed it to him. What he caught was a live, unhappy, snake. He thrust the snake at the man's face. "Lie and the snake will strike. The poison is swift, but extremely painful, especially in the area of the genitals." He lowered the snake down the man's body. "Now, where is she?"

"238 Merchant street," babbled the man, trying to turn his face away. Viper dropped him.

"Shadow."

"Yes?"

"These people all wear the tattoos of the gang you first encountered in this realm. There is only one way to earn that mark."

"Understood. Let's go." As she started towards the door she called the dragon. "Aeroth!" The serpentine beast materialized in the shadows. "Destroy them all." She didn't look back a single time until the screams stopped. The dragon, blood dripping from its jaws, appeared from the door. It turned then sent a gout of fire into the house, engulfing it in flames. With a defiant scream it leaped into the air and disappeared. The big car roared to life and sped away.

ELLEN SLOWLY CAME BACK to consciousness. She groaned and that earned her a slap across the mouth. "Shut up, bitch. We got no time for this."

"Hey, Pick, go easy. You heard what the fed said. He wants her in one piece."

"Yeah, well, what for?"

"She's that Shadow woman's bitch. Linwood's going use her to make the Shadow do what we want."

At that Ellen chuckled. "You poor fools. You have no idea what you're messing with, but you'll find out before you die."

"I said shut up, bitch." The blow didn't land as his partner caught his wrist. "I said go easy, Pick. We fucked up bad here."

"Huh? What're you talking about? How did we mess up?"

"Listen, I got a bad feeling about this. How did we get this job? We're not even in the gang yet."

"Okay, so, how about we use this one? She's already here."

The second man, barely more than a boy, began pacing around. "Man, you're so stupid; I can't believe you're my brother. We can't use her, moron. If we mess her up that fed'll kill the both of us."

"All right, so let's go grab another one."

"We can't do that either. Linwood said to lay low, keep her out of sight until he calls."

"Well shit, we gotta do something. If we been set up, then what? We should run."

"We do that then we have the fed, Shadow, and the whole gang after us."

"So tell me, boys, how did you decide I was Lady Shadow's girlfriend?"

"We been watching you for weeks, bitch. We seen you and that other bitch kissing like two lezzie hoes. We..." The phone rang in his pocket. He snatched it out and answered. "Yo. Hello? Gina??" He dropped the phone as that cold voice spoke. Ellen heard it and so did the other man. "Gina is dead." terrified, he backed away from the phone. "As will you be soon."

"Oh, shit. Oh, Jesus."

"Too late to start praying now, little man," said Ellen. "Your time's about up."

"She won't be so damn tough with a gun to your head, bitch."

"You're just making it worse and wasting time. Shadow's on her way. The only chance you two misfits have is to run."

"Shut up, woman. Just shut the fuck up. I need to think."

"You do that, it should be a new experience for you."

He spun around and pointed a gun at her head. His hand was shaking. Ellen swallowed hard. She was afraid she had pushed him too far. Finally he lowered the gun. "We should phone Linwood."

"Are you kidding me? Do you remember what happened to the last guy who didn't do what he was told? He said not to call until he did."

"While you're thinking about your options, there's something else you might want to consider."

He turned to Ellen with murder in his eyes. "Just what would that be?"

"Viper."

"Oh, shit. Oh no, no, no," said the second man. "I'm done here. I am out of here. I..." there was a rumble, then the scream of a high-powered engine outside. "Hey, it's the guys. I knew we'd get some back up. I... Oh fuck. It's the Viper and the woman. We ..." He got no further as the door exploded inward. Viper stepped inside and fired twice. Both men fell to the floor twitching then lay still.

Shadow already had Ellen free of the bonds and held tightly in her arms. She carried her outside then called out. "Aeroth." The dragon appeared and Shadow placed Ellen on its back then climbed up behind her. "Take us home, my pet."

As the dragon flew away with his riders the Viper checked his weapons carefully then got back in his car. The next morning it was all over the news. The vigilante known as Viper had gone on a rampage during the night. Three known gang houses had been hit and the body count was over eighteen. He'd set the houses on fire to burn the drugs and bodies. It was a police nightmare.

Hard Target

Ellen was quite shaky by the time they arrived back at the condo. Seline brought her a big glass of wine, then set about fixing the locks on the door. Ellen watched as she fussed with the locks then called the dragon to stand guard. "Seline honey, can I ask a question?"

"Sure love, what's on your mind?"

"Aeroth, he's actually real?"

"Yes, as real as anything else. We are all made of energy and..."

"Okay, I get the basic science. It's just that sometimes he's so big, yet he can walk through doors, and he can fly, but..."

"According to physics he shouldn't be able to with the wing size to body ratio?"

"Yeah, that."

"Same thing for the bumble bee and the humming birds flying backwards. There's a rational explanation for it, but I have no idea what it is. I just know he can fly, and I feel safe on his back. So, what are we really doing here? Displacement activity?"

"Yeah, that," replied Ellen, trying to steady the shaking in her hand. "My god, those guys, they weren't even in the gang, but they were willing to..."

"Hey now, you're safe. I'm here and those guys are gone forever." Seline was cuddling Ellen against her belly, lightly stroking her hair.

Ellen gave her a gentle squeeze around the waist then released her. "There'll be more. They've actually been watching us for weeks. How? And how did we not know?"

"Questions for tomorrow, my lover," smiled Seline. "Come on. I'm tucking you into bed and I'll hold you close all night so you will sleep in safety. Tomorrow we'll deal with the unanswered questions."

The next morning Seline arose to find herself alone in the bed. She went downstairs to find Ellen hard at work on her laptop. "Hi there, gorgeous, sleep well?"

"I slept like a baby in your arms, my darling." Ellen hadn't raised her head from the computer.

"Whatcha doin'?"

"Preemptive strike, battening down the hatches, manning the walls, and bracing the gates."

"Okay, have fun with that." Seline poured a coffee then retreated to the living room where she found the dragon resting, yet still alert. "Go to your rest, my pet. I'm up." The huge beast nuzzled at her hand, then vanished.

Seline settled into her chair then closed her eyes. "Lady Moragah?"

"*I am here, Lady Shadow. What troubles you?*"

"I'm just trying to wrap my head around a few things. I know I have to put aside all I learned before we met ..."

"*But still you are troubled.*"

"I just can't seem to tell the good guys from the bad guys anymore."

"*You must release those old concepts, Seline. A human government will define who are the good guys. Any who oppose them are labeled the bad guys.*"

"Okay, so who are we supposed to be, good guys or bad guys?"

"*You are my children. You are the defenders of the weak. You operate outside the constraints of the old idea, you look past the surface of what you see, you drive back the darkness and defend the weak. The concepts of right and wrong, good guy, bad guy, are no longer relevant to your purpose in life.*

"*Seline, there must always be balance in the universe, light and dark, good and bad, etc. I became involved again when I met Penny. I gave her the means to defend the weak. Kara as well. Sadly, I could not ignore the encroaching darkness. Things in this realm are too far out of balance and getting worse. I changed things a bit when I augmented Tasha. Still, the darkness marches onward."*

"So that's why you gave me even greater powers?"

"Yes, for your task is greater. The others deal with whatever presents itself to them. You, my dear priestess, are the huntress. You must seek out the bringers of darkness and stop them."

"So I'm working at a different level?"

"Correct. The old ways of thinking, the laws, and concepts have no meaning for you now. You are a bringer of balance, a law unto yourself. Your purpose is to push back the darkness. You may use whatever methods you desire."

"Moragah?"

"Forgive me, Seline. I trust in your better nature to find a way to push back the darkness, defend the weak, and retain your humanity at the same time. I will assist you all I can. Seline, I am well pleased with you and the way you are growing into your role, your purpose."

"I scared myself a bit last night."

"I know, but you remained in control and did what was needed. Seline, I love your natural compassion, but I am also thrilled that you can set it aside in time of need. Those who lost their lives last night had already embraced the darkness. To let them continue would have unleashed untold misery on the innocent, the weaker members of this society. You have only done what I ask of you, and you have done it well. Do not doubt yourself, my daughter."

With that, Moragah sent a wave of healing energy through Seline, bringing a smile to her lips. "Thank you, Mother Goddess."

"Talking to Moragah?" asked Ellen, as she joined Seline in the living room.

"Yeah, just trying to get my head straight. When the action starts I tend to run on instinct, but afterwards I come apart."

"I know, sweetie. Mother Moragah make it all better?"

"She made a few things clearer."

"Such as?"

"The governments and religions define who the good guys and the bad guys are, but it isn't necessarily so."

"Second that."

"Yeah, well, Moragah defined us for me. We aren't the good guys in the traditional sense, neither are we the bad guys as the government and media will portray us. We're the children of Moragah, defenders of the weak, defiers of the darkness. Neither good guys nor bad guys, yet we will be seen as both."

Ellen just nodded, absorbing the new information and accepting it, as well as her role in it all.

"So, what were you up to over there?" asked Seline.

"Putting an emergency backup plan into motion."

"Backup plan? Care to share?"

"Honey, you've beaten these guys every time they came at you. I expect them to get pissed about it soon. I expect them to come at us full force any day now."

"Full force?"

"Bust down the door, drag us away for a grilling or worse. Cancel our P.I. license, freeze our bank accounts, seize our assets, and accuse us of terrorism; allowing them to lock us away forever, never to be heard from again."

"Ellen, I will never allow that to happen."

"Girl, I have every faith you can bust us out if we get grabbed, but a life on the run with no funds or resources is not a gig I'm anxious to embrace. I've created new identities for us and squirreled away enough money to keep us comfortable for years. If they freeze our assets we can still tap into the backup funds using the new identities."

"Cool. Woman, you're awesome. How do you do that anyway, create new identities that don't get busted."

"Oh, they won't stand up to heavy scrutiny, but first you have to know who to scrutinize. You can change your appearance at will. I can dye my hair, wear glasses, and change my clothing style. Now, it will take me most of the day to finalize this. What are you planning for today?"

"Riding shotgun for you. We can send Vic to locate Linwood. You know, we should include Debbie and Vic in our backup plan if possible."

"Already done. Sweetheart, I know you love this condo, but we really should think about moving to more secure digs."

"More secure? You mean like a penthouse in a secure building, a warehouse with an apartment and an electric fence, or maybe ...?"

"Something along those lines. It's just that our offices and this place have been under surveillance for weeks. That makes me nervous."

"Yeah, me too. Okay, whatever you think is best. Wherever we go should have easy and discrete access and exits for us hunted criminal types, and yet secure against invaders. Something like the Bat Cave."

"Yeah, something like that. I'll work on it, that's my job."

"And I'll ride shotgun for you until Vic locates Linwood. Once we can pin him down I'll take him out. That bastard will pay for hurting you."

"Easy, girl," smiled Ellen, as she rose, crossed to Seline's chair then slid into her lap. "I'm okay. You rescued me in time. No harm done and the kidnappers paid the price."

Seline hugged her gently. "No, girl, those fools were just pawns in the game. Linwood is the man behind it. He wanted to use you to bring me under his thumb."

Ellen took Seline's face in both her hands, gazing into the girl's eyes. "That could never happen, and I know it full well. If something like that should ever come to pass, you can't give in. You have to do what Moragah would need you to do. I know this, Seline, my lover. I know and I'm fully prepared to face that day if I have to."

"Ellen ..."

"Well, it sure as hell isn't plan A, girl."

Seline laughed and buried her nose in Ellen's ribs, causing her to shriek. "No, it isn't plan A, and it's a hell of a long way down the list."

"What? Seline, what just crossed your mind just then?"

"Plan B. It needs a bit of work, but I think I have a plan B in my head now."

"Care to share?"

"Later, my love. Let me get it worked into shape a bit first. Come on, let's go out for breakfast, then get on with your backup plan."

At the office Ellen informed her best detective, Dave, that he might get a call at any time to take over the office until further notice. He didn't argue or say anything. He'd known for a while something big was in the wind. After that, Ellen called Debbie and Victor in to confer with her and Seline. She explained her backup plan and suggested they do something similar. Debbie grinned as she told them she already had it in the works.

Victor noticed Seline watching him. "What?"

"I saw the news this morning."

"Yeah? Anything interesting happen?"

"It was good work. What the Viper did was necessary. Just wanted you to know." He nodded and smiled shyly. "Now, I need you to locate Linwood. For the love of god, Vic, be careful. The bastard has spies everywhere. Just find him, don't try to take him down."

"This one personal?"

"Damn right it is."

"Fair enough. I'll find him for you, but I get to ride shotgun when you go in."

Five days later, they caught up with him at the office near the docks. "Yes, he's in there," said Shadow. "I can hear him on the phone."

"And there's no one else?"

"No, he's alone."

"Why does this smell like a trap?"

"Because it probably is a trap. Stay sharp."

"Yes, ma'am, eyes peeled and alert." As he spoke the magic armor encased his body and he pulled out his guns.

"Okay, let's go." She led the way, but found the main door locked. Shadow made easy work of that. It took only moments to find the office, but the closer they got the more her instincts shrieked at her to run.

"Damn, Shadow, this place is creeping me out," whispered Viper.

"He's alone in there. This is definitely a trap. The bastard is looking right at us and grinning."

"Screw this," snarled Viper, as he took a step forward, spun around and lashed out with a big boot. The door exploded inward in splinters. They both leaped through.

Linwood was at a back door, holding up a device. Laughing he activated it and fled, slamming the steel door behind him.

"Bomb!" shouted, Viper as he threw himself in front of Shadow. The world shattered around him in a wall of sound and destruction. Viper found himself on the floor holding his ears and moaning. Lady Shadow lay still beside him. Something else was wrong. He wasn't bleeding and there was no pain except for his ears.

His foot touched something and he spun around. "A wall," he said in amazement. There was a concrete wall. Somehow she had materialized a wall to protect them from the blast. Viper struggled to his feet, then scooped Shadow gently into his arms and carried her back to the car.

Ellen answered the door to find Viper, still in his armor and holding an unconscious Shadow in his arms. She stepped aside, her hand over her mouth as he entered. "I think she's okay," he said, as he laid her on the sofa. "There was a bomb. She managed to make a wall to protect us, but I think it took the good out of her."

"Oh fuck, my head hurts," came a soft moan from the couch. "Anybody get the number of the truck that hit me?"

"Yeah, I got it," grinned Viper, as his armor vanished. Ellen was now cradling Seline in her arms, whispering soothing sounds. "Next time make some hearing protection along with the wall."

"The wall worked?"

"Sure did, Shadow. You rock, woman."

"Linwood?"

"Bastard got away. Ellen, got any aspirin? I think both of us could use it."

"Over the bathroom sink, there," she replied, as she pointed the way. He nodded. A moment later he was back with the aspirin and water for Seline. He collapsed into a chair as she took it.

"Vic, are you all right?" asked Ellen.

"Yeah, just beat. Look, I know that using the magic takes the starch out of Shadow. Making that wall must have cost her big time. She'll need to rest a few days. I'll go catch a few hours sleep then go back on the hunt for Linwood. That fucker just rubbed my fur the wrong way."

"Vic, you be careful," said Seline, her voice weak. "Next time we play the game differently. Just locate him."

"But I want to shoot him," said Vic, a grin on his face.

"Go home, Vic. Get some sleep," smiled Ellen. "I'll tuck this poor girl in for the night then stand guard."

"You think he'll come here?" asked Viper, the armor back on.

"Won't chance it."

"Aeroth will watch," sighed Seline. She closed her eyes again as the serpentine beast came from the shadows. Viper gave them a salute then stepped out the door.

Resettlement/New Tactics

Seline slept through much of the day, then went to bed early. Ellen stayed with her, working at her computer and making phone calls, but Seline was too tired to pay attention. She simply slept or drifted through the worlds of her imagination. As she did so, her plan B came into tighter focus. So did her acceptance of who she was becoming and what Moragah wanted from her.

Late on the second day, Ellen found her in the library, reading. She was in Shadow mode. "Well, looks like my warrior princess is back. How are you feeling?"

"Much better," replied Seline. She set the bookmark, then closed the book and set it on the table beside her chair. "So, tell me what you've been up to while I was sleeping off the bomb hangover."

Ellen kissed her cheek, then took the chair beside her, folding her legs under her. "Well, I've been shopping, so to speak. It took a bit, but I have a new home for us, new office building as well."

"Oh?"

"Yes, we can move to the new place and set up, then we can sell this place and the current business to recoup the cost."

"Wait, what? Sell the business?"

"Yes, Dave will buy it, he's said so many times. We'll set up a new investigation business, taking only exclusive clients. It'll cut down our workload and allow us to focus more on Moragah's purpose."

"Ellen, are you sure?"

"I'm sure, sweetie. We'll keep Debbie and Vic on staff of course. After all, they're family."

Seline smiled at that. "Okay, can we afford to do this?"

"Yes, easily. It's already in the works."

"You're angry."

"Yes, I am. I'm angry at myself for being so careless that I nearly comprised you, got myself kidnapped, and worst of all, we were being watched and I didn't pick up on it. I promise you, that will not happen again."

"Oh, I love it when you get all fierce." Seline gave Ellen a lascivious look and licked her lips.

"Later, my mad fool, later," laughed Ellen. "Right now we have to focus. I need to show you something before I finalize the purchase."

"Oh? What are we buying?"

"A new home. Come on, We'll go pick up the keys and look the place over."

They drove to a real estate office where Ellen picked up the keys, telling them she was representing a reclusive client who wished to remain anonymous. Once she had the keys she drove to an exclusive neighborhood. A touch of the remote and the gate swung open. Beyond the gate, a wide driveway led into a forest, dipping down to become invisible from the street. It turned sharply, then rose again to the mansion. Mansion? It looked more like a fortress.

The house was huge, built of stone and concrete. Ellen explained it once belonged to a crime family. The doors and windows were bullet proof and the walls two feet thick. Seline followed Ellen as they explored the house, her eyes wide with wonder. Damn, even though it had obviously been empty for many years the place was still magnificent.

Ellen checked some papers as they made their way back to the ground floor. "This way." She led Seline towards the back to a private office. It was still furnished as it had been many years before. "Now, where is that ... Ah, here it is." She touched a switch under the surface of the desk and a bookcase swung away from the wall. Behind it was a stairway. She flicked on the lights, and they went down.

"This part of the basement is separate from the rest. The laundry area, wine cellar, and other amenities are beyond that wall. This room will do fine as an armory. Now, through this door is access to the second garage."

"Second garage?" asked Seline, as she followed Ellen through the door into a three car garage.

"Yes, the main garage is one floor up and will hold eight cars. This one holds three and opens onto another driveway that empties onto a service road for the forestry people. This property backs onto a park."

"Bolt hole."

"Exactly. There's more. A secure panic room is also built into the basement. It has everything we'd need to survive for weeks."

"Holy crap. Ellen, how did you ever find this place?" Ellen didn't respond, nor did she make eye contact. "Ellen?"

"My grandfather and his brothers built it," she said at last. "The family has been trying to get rid of it for years. They don't want any connection to the past. I contacted them asking for anonymity. I bought it under my new name. I'll get a cleaning crew in here tomorrow, then go sign the papers. We should be able to move in in a couple of weeks."

"Holy crap. Ellen, this is awesome. We can get Vic to help us move. He can do the heavy lifting."

"We'll hire a moving company for that, sweetie. However, you'll have to change your appearance and work with them."

"Not a problem."

"So, you're okay with it? With the history of the place?"

"Oh hell yeah, it's perfect."

Ellen smiled at last. "Okay then, shall we go home and see if Vic has located Linwood yet?"

"Good plan, let's go."

LINWOOD WAS LAYING low, having discovered his bomb had failed. He also needed to recruit new people for the street. Viper had seriously thinned out his contacts and workforce. He stayed on the move and slept in a different place every night. He was on the run and he didn't like it. As soon as his new agents arrived he planned to turn the tables on Shadow and Viper. He had to get them off his back.

For his part, Victor was getting frustrated. This keeping a low profile and playing the coward was wearing on his nerves. He began to spend more and more time working on his secret apartment. It was in the building next to where he hid the Vipermobile. His stepfather owned both buildings and he was supposed to be looking after them. He was. They'd make a perfect hideout for the Viper.

It took nearly a month for it all to fall into place. Vic was already moved into his new apartment, and it was the day before the movers were to arrive at Ellen's condo. Ellen checked her computer over morning coffee as was her habit. Suddenly she began to curse.

"Ellen, what is it?" asked Seline as she hurried into the kitchen.

"It's happened. The bastards have seized our assets and ..." the door was suddenly assaulted. "All right, all right, leave some paint on it," she shouted, as she went to answer the insistent pounding. She swept it open with a harsh demand. "Who are you and what do you want?"

"Are you Ellen Cameron?" demanded a heavyset man in a cheap suit.

"Yes, what do you want?"

"This is a warrant," he replied, slapping her chest with a large envelope. "Your P.I. license is hereby suspended. Your office is being seized and I'm authorized to confiscate any and all files you may have on these premises. Your assets have been frozen, and you're under arrest on charges of terrorism." He grabbed her and spun her around then his world went all to hell.

Seline didn't bother to change or to call the dragon. She moved with the speed of a tigress, slamming her fist into the man's jaw, and sending him to the floor, unconscious. She grabbed his partner and threw the man against the wall. He went for his gun but she slapped it away. She then hurled him across the room, where he landed on his companion bringing a groan of protest. Seline was on them again. They found themselves against the wall, their guns trained on them and an angry Seline holding said guns.

"All right," she said, a snarl on her lips, "now that I have your attention, listen up. You two assholes are in way over your heads. You go back to Linwood and tell him what happened here. Tell him I'm coming for him. I will find him, I will kill him, but in my own time and in my own way. If either of you idiots come at me again you'll just be collateral damage. Now get the hell out of my house." She tossed the guns behind her and pushed the two men towards the door.

They left, hurriedly, glancing fearfully over their shoulders. "Ellen honey, is there any chance the movers could come today?"

"Working on it." A few minutes later she lowered her phone. "They'll be here in an hour with an unmarked truck."

"Oh?"

"A man owes me a favor. He'll do the move, and nobody will ever know where we went."

"Good. You take care of the move. I have business elsewhere."

Ellen crossed the floor to put her arms around the angry young woman. "Seline, where are you going?"

"Washington."

"Why?"

"Because I'm sick of playing around with this. They want to bring the heat? I'll give them heat."

"Seline, listen to me now. Listen. Wait for me. I'll go with you."

"No, Ellen, this could be ..."

"Yes, Lady Shadow. You need a day to clear your head and to make a plan. You will also need a getaway driver. Wait for me."

"You won't try to talk me out of this?"

"No. You're going after the director of the CIA, aren't you?"

"Yep."

"It won't do any good, they'll just appoint someone else."

"I'm not going to kill him, lover." Seline relaxed in Ellen's arms at last. "I'm just going to get these morons off our backs. By the time I'm done with him they'll want no part of us."

"Just what are you up to?"

"Plan B. I'm building an alternate world in my mind. I'll take him there and threaten to leave him if he doesn't get these assholes under control. This scare tactics and disappear forever crap can work both ways. I plan to see how he likes it."

"You'll never get close to him."

"No, but one of his agents just might."

"Agents? Which one?"

"Terrance. If I can't make that work I'll think of something else, but this has to happen. You're right, if I kill him they'll just make another. I think it'll be better all the way around if this one makes it easier for me to operate. Trust me, the director is going off world, then our lives are getting easier."

The two agents reported to Linwood, and he just laughed. "Get a truck and clean out their offices," he said. "That'll piss them off. Then we'll get the local cops to take them down." They proceeded with their orders, but were stymied there are well. There was a lawyer with a cease and desist order waiting for them. It seemed the woman had sold her business to one of her detectives and the warrant couldn't be served.

Frustrated, they returned to Linwood's new office, requisitioned new weapons, then headed for the police station. By the time they arrived at the condo with a SWAT team, the place was empty. No one knew where they'd gone, the truck hadn't had any signs on it. Linwood was with them, and he wasn't happy. "An unmarked truck. Goddamn son of a bitch, they could be anywhere. Get an APB out on those two. I want them found."

It wasn't going to be that easy. At the new house the girls were unpacking. The sports car and Old Betsy were already tucked into the huge garage and covered with tarps. "We're going to need new wheels," said Seline, as she began loading up the bookshelves.

Ellen stopped and smiled at her. "Yes, we will, but that can wait for tomorrow. So, what sort of car do you want? Something like's Vic's viper?"

Seline laughed and shook her head. "It sure is sexy all right, but no. That's his deal. No, we need two. Something like Old Betsy and something sweet to drive for fun."

"Okay, we'll work on it, see what's out there. First, however, since I'm not gifted like my lover, I'll have to spend some time on my disguise. I need to get my hair dyed, tinted contacts or glasses. Maybe I should paint a tooth black, what do you think?"

"Me? What do I think? How about this?" Seline waved her hand and Ellen felt a tingle run through her.

She stepped over to a large mirror and gasped. Her skin was darker, her hair long and jet black, and her eyes a deep liquid brown. "Wow." She ran her hands over her face then Seline grinned wickedly and waved again. Now Ellen was a platinum blonde with a deep tan, her eyes a piercing blue. Seline gave her a moment to look it over then giggled and waved her hand again. This time Ellen was the red haired girl Seline had teased her with.

Ellen's laugh was full and rich. "So, it's really you who has a thing for the red-haired girl."

She noticed Seline's head cocked to one side as though listening. Suddenly Seline's smile brightened. "So, which one do you like, or would you like to try something else different?"

"Seline?"

"Moragah let me give Vic armor. She thinks the disguise for you would be the same thing. She likes the idea. So, tell me who you want to be, and we'll make that happen for you."

"Are you serious?"

"Yes, ma'am. So, what will it be?"

"How about I do the blonde and you do the red-haired girl."

"There, I knew it, you do have a thing for the redheads."

"Shut up. God, Seline, you're a nut. So how do I do this?"

"First get a clear picture in your mind of how she looked. Then see her in the mirror. I'll help you for the first few times."

Thus it began. Ellen was a quick study and within two days she was popping back and forth between herself and the blonde with ease. The third day she spent all day in disguise. On day four they set out for Washington driving their new Mercedes. They arrived late and spent the night in an expensive hotel. The next morning they began their search. Two days later, they had the director's office, phone number, and his home address.

They sat in the car, within easy reach of the man's gate. There was plenty of security, tall gate, cameras,etc. "So, any idea how you want to do this?" asked Ellen.

"We're good here," replied Seline. "I'm not taking any chances with this guy. I thought about doing the Terrance thing, but that would put me too close to him. We'll stay right here in the car. When he stops to open his gate I'll take him. After that bomb I'm being extra cautious. We'll just stay here, and I'll do it all through illusion. After all, I don't want to kill the guy, just scare the crap out of him."

"Can you do that? All through illusion?"

"Pretty sure I can. Remember Daniels? This will be the same thing. It's a hot day, he should have the windows down. While he's out of it, you go put this note in his pocket, while I've got him off world I'll put a note in his pocket. He'll wake up, try to convince himself it was all an hallucination, then he'll find the note. That will convince him it was all real. Don't worry, the security cameras will see nothing but a deep fog the whole time."

"Okay, sounds good. Girl, if this goes sideways ..."

"If that happens, I'll call the dragon and we'll fly away. Let them figure that out. Whoops, here he comes. Make like you're on the phone."

A car drove by, a man in his sixties at the wheel. He glanced at them, but Ellen was having an animated conversation with her phone, ignoring him completely. He continued on to his driveway, stopping to open the gate. As he reached for the remote his world went all to hell. A dark mist descended, enveloping the car, and then he wasn't in the car anymore.

Suddenly terrified, the man reached for his gun and his phone. He found neither. He shouted for help and a light appeared. A woman of incredible beauty came towards him. She was tall and appeared to be an African tribeswoman. "Please help me."

"Yes, I have come to guide you," she said, extending her hand. As she spoke the mist pulled back to reveal the walls of a tunnel. "Come this way. Be careful not to touch the walls. They can be very dangerous."

He took her hand, clinging tightly. "Where are we? What's happening?"

"You've been summoned by Lady Shadow. I'm here to guide you to her, and again on your return journey, should you be returning." He started to ask another question, but they had reached the end of the tunnel. "She awaits you there."

She pointed to a jumble of boulders overlooking a ruined city. All the buildings were broken, some smoking still. A woman dressed in leather armor stood with her back to him, gazing out over the scene of destruction. He noticed her up-swept ears and long red braid. She turned to him with a smile that did not reach her eyes. It displayed her fangs and that sent a shiver down his spine.

He approached her cautiously. "Who are you? What do you want? Why have you brought me to this place?"

"Careful of the snakes." She used her staff to flick a small snake away from his shoe. "Their venom is powerful and swift. One bite and you have only a moment to live." He swallowed hard and froze in place, his eyes fearfully sweeping the ground. "Come close to me."

Cautiously, he obeyed. As he reached her side she swept her hand out in a wide gesture indicating he should look at the ruined city. He saw the shattered buildings more clearly now. It must have been incredibly beautiful at one time. Now it lay in ruins, bombed into rubble, or so he imagined. Looking closer he could see figures moving about. They appeared to be soldiers of some kind, wearing armor, and carrying weapons he didn't recognize.

"What happened here?" he asked softly.

"Men like you listened to the dark fears in their cowardly minds. The Darkness gained full control and they rose up against each other until this is all that remains. Look closely, you can see two distinct species." He nodded. Both species were vaguely humanoid, but distinctly different. As soon as one spotted one of the others it attacked. They fought until one was dead.

"There aren't many left on either side, but they pay no heed to survival, not of the body nor for their own species. The darkness has completely engulfed them. The only thought that remains to them is to destroy the other. In this place, the Darkness has overcome the Light. This is the result."

"Why have you brought me here? Why have you shown me this?"

"I have two reasons. Sit." She indicated a boulder for him, and she sat facing him.

"First, I want you to listen to me. I thought I'd have a far better chance of holding your attention here instead of your office. You, and those like you, are far too paranoid to listen to reason unless forced to do so. This world is a result of the Darkness and Light getting too far out of balance. Your own world sits on the brink of this fate. I was sent to your world to help restore the balance. I want your help to accomplish this.

"I enlisted a woman of your species to help me, however, men who report to you have visited great harm upon her. They have taken her assets, removed her ability to earn her way in the world, and attempted to kidnap her. I stopped that. I have become quite fond of this woman and want her protected. I also want your people to cease importing and selling body poisons in your home country."

"What? Look, I have no knowledge of any wrong doing by any of my ... Ahh!" He flailed wildly at the small viper which had sunk its fangs into his leg. He started to faint.

"Quickly, drink this, every drop of it." He snatched the vial from her hand and drank it greedily. His vision began to clear instantly. She gave him a moment then bent down to scoop the tiny snake up in her elegant fingers. She stroked its head fondly then set it back on the ground. "That was the last of the antidote. I have no more with me so be careful what you say. This one is Trix; he hates it when people lie to me. And he always knows."

The man swallowed hard, his eyes wide with fear, his hands trembling. He nodded his acquiescence.

"As I said, I want that practice stopped. I know that you probably can't stop it, but I can. I will slowly work my way up through your chain of command, eliminating agents as I go, until I succeed. Your task is to make certain it doesn't start up again. However, your first task is to ensure my friend is restored, her funds and assets returned, her license to practice returned, and your people to understand she is out of bounds. She must not be harmed or hindered.

"The second reason I brought you here is to leave you behind if you refuse to comply." He was trembling in terror as he looked past her shoulder. The huge serpentine beast stepped closer, then gently nuzzled at her neck. She reached up to pet it affectionately. "This one is Aeroth. He is friendly enough, but his brethren are not.

"So, enough time has been lost here. Give me your decision, will you comply with my wishes, or shall I leave you here and offer the bargain to the next man in your position?"

"No, no, please, don't leave me here," he begged, as he grasped at her arm. The dragon hissed at him and he released her, shrinking away from the glittering eyes of the beast.

"Well?"

"Yes, yes, it's a deal. I'll call them off. Please, don't leave me here."

"Very well then, this is the woman's name and address." She tucked a note in the pocket of his jacket. "This woman will lead you back to your world."

He turned to find the African woman holding her hand out to him. He grasped her hand tightly and followed her. The tunnel reappeared and they entered. Soon they reached the fog and suddenly he was alone.

Terrified, he froze in place. A moment later he realized the fog was gone and he was back in his car. He felt something in his pocket and pulled it out. It was the paper with a woman's name and address on it. Ellen Cameron, Private Detective. He swallowed hard and pulled out his phone.

"OKAY, HE'S GOT THE note, now what? Do we trust him and go home?"

"I don't trust any of these guys as far as you could throw them."

Ellen chuckled at that. "Me neither. Let's go back to the hotel and relax. Give him a couple of days to get things done then check up. What do we do if he double crosses us?"

"If he does, I'll take him down in the night and we go after the next one. Sooner or later one of these guys will be smart enough to take the deal."

Seline's voice trailed off as she snuggled down the seat. "My poor darling," smiled Ellen, "you're all tuckered out. I'll get you back to the hotel and tuck you into bed."

Seline fairly purred. "Mmm, I like that idea."

WITH A SOFT GROAN OF delight Seline rolled over and stretched. She heard the sound of fingers on keyboard and looked to see Ellen hard at work. The hotel room had a small table and Ellen had turned it into a desk. Seline smiled with delight as she watched her lover and mentor working.

Ellen heard her and looked up with a smile. "Good afternoon, Miss Sleepyhead. Feeling better?"

"Afternoon?" Seline sat up and tousled her hair. "How long was I out?"

"Close to sixteen hours."

"Holy smokes, that long? I'll admit, that did take the good out of me. It's actually easier if I'm physically there in the illusion with them."

"One less image to project?"

"Ah-huh, that and less distance to project over. The distance thing is hard because I have to leave the space between us normal. Any idea if it worked yet?"

With a bright smile Ellen rose from the chair and stretched. "Yes, it worked. By ten this morning, our bank accounts were unfrozen and the P.I. license was restored. By noon somebody had set our old condo on fire."

"What? Seriously?"

"Yep."

"Damn that Linwood, the man has no sense of humor at all. Thank god we got the library moved. Any word from the kids?"

"Debbie is having fun playing house in Vic's new apartment, but he's starting to get twitchy."

Seline yawned then climbed to her feet. "I guess it's time for us to go home then. Our work here is done for the moment."

Ellen stepped close then hugged her tightly. "My poor girl, you're still not back to a hundred percent. Let's get you in the shower then check out, grab a meal, then hit the road for home. You can nap while I drive."

"Deal," Seline murmured from Ellen's shoulder. Ellen barely felt the soft kiss just below her ear. "Can I have an appetizer in the shower?"

"That depends," replied Ellen, tilting her head back to make it easier for Seline to plan soft kisses on her neck.

"On what?" asked Seline, placing light kisses on the offered neck.

"Who do I get, Seline or the red-haired girl?"

"You can have both if you want," giggled Seline as she began nuzzling at Ellen's cleavage.

Ellen laughed with delight. "Deal." She took Seline's hand and led her to the shower. It was late in the evening before they arrived back at the hidden mansion.

The Hunt for Linwood

O nce again, Seline slept late, but this time she awakened fully refreshed. She was alone in the bedroom, so she quickly dressed and hurried downstairs where she found Ellen, Debbie, and Victor setting up the office in what had once been a large study. "Oh, thank god," grinned Vic, "somebody to help me with the heavy lifting."

"Aw, Vic, you missed me," grinned Seline. "What are we lifting?"

"These danged file cabinets. They're full. The boys at the old office helped me load them, but ..." With a delighted laugh, Seline followed him out to the rental truck. Once the super woman got involved the work went a lot faster. Soon they were standing back admiring their handiwork.

"So what are we going to use for a reception area?" asked Debbie.

"There won't be one," replied Ellen. "This arrangement will work well to allow us to do what we must and easily interact with each other. The idea for this new agency is simple; the client contacts us, we go to them. We're super hush-hush, under the radar so people can feel easy about hiring us."

"They'll be assured of complete anonymity; no one will ever spot them entering our office?"

"Right, and nobody will ever know where our office is. I don't ever want a repeat of Mrs. Alldon."

Debbie reached out to give Ellen's arm a gentle squeeze. "I hear that, and I fully agree. Considering who we're working with, that will always be a danger."

Vic nodded his agreement. "Yeah, well, I may have our first customer. However, I'd like Shadow to do the initial interview."

Seline quirked an eyebrow at him. "Why?"

"It's the chief of police. I was in the station, just idly poking around and he approached me. Actually, he read me the riot act about interfering in ongoing investigations. That was just an excuse. He dragged me into his office, bawling at me the whole time, then he quietly asked me if we could look into something for him. I said I'd check and let him know if Ellen's interested."

Ellen smiled. "This could be our big break. Let's see what he wants. If it's worth doing, and we get it right, he could throw us a lot of work, as well as be a possible source of inside information in the future. Seline?"

"Oh yeah, I'm all over this. There's a coffee shop near the station. Let me get into position then tell him to meet me there. Tell him to look for a redhead with freckles." Grinning, she morphed into her new disguise, wearing a police uniform."

"Nice touch," grinned Victor. "Buzz me where you're ready."

"Okay. Ellen, wire me up."

"Excuse me?"

"I want you to be able to hear everything and also give me questions to ask."

"Right. Now, that stuff was all in the..."

"Here," said Debbie, as she opened the appropriate file cabinet. A few moments later, Vic made his call as Ellen and Seline drove away.

THE CHIEF OF POLICE sighed as he took his coffee and danish to a corner booth. The cafe was quiet at this time of day. A moment later he was joined by a young woman in a police uniform. The girl had red hair and freckles. She winked at him and slid a business card across the table as she took a sip of her coffee. "You were looking for me?"

"Seline Elmore," he said as he read the card. "So, you're Walsh's new boss?"

"I work for. She's out of town right now, so I'm up. How can we help?"

"Look, this has to stay under the radar, if you know what I mean."

"Absolutely. Our new agency has no offices, and we keep no incriminating files. However, since that makes billing an issue, we are careful who we choose to work for."

"I'm not a rich man ..."

"Understood. If we decide to take this case it'll be as a gesture of good will. Chief, you're going to have to trust us and we, in turn, are going to have to trust you."

"I don't like the sound of that. What is this going to really cost me."

"I'm sure you're aware of the fact we've been the target of harassment by a certain government agency recently. All we're asking for is a heads up in case anything like this is going to happen again."

"Give you a chance to blow town?"

"Call it what you want. The alternative is financial. Two thousand a day, plus expenses. Four day minimum and half up front. No receipts, no refunds."

"I don't have that kind of money. Shit. All right, I'm desperate here. I'll take option one, but I warn you, I won't be a bottomless pit of police favors."

"Fair enough, but there's this speeding ticket..."

"Oh, for Christ's sake."

"Lighten up, Chief. Just kidding. So, what's the job?"

"The city is drowning in drugs, we've been warned off any and all investigations, as well as other activities. My town has been ripped away from me, leaving it wide open and me helpless to do my job."

"What do you need from us?"

"I need to know who's pulling the strings and how to stop them."

"Easy money, Chief. The puppet master locally is CIA agent Linwood."

"Linwood?"

"Shhh, keep your voice down or he'll find out and make you disappear. That bastard's got spies everywhere and he's after my hide."

"You? Why?"

"I messed up his mojo a few months ago. I've been laying low ever since."

"Okay, so how do I stop the bastard?"

"Just be patient. The man has enemies."

"Oh?"

"Lady Shadow and the Viper are looking for him. Once they find him I don't give a lot for his chances.

"Lady Shadow, you mean you."

"Me? You think I'm Shadow?"

"Aren't you? She always seems to show up when you're around. Don't try to deny it. You tossed those two feds around like superman. You just have to be Shadow."

"Yeah, when was this?"

"You know damn well it was last week."

"I was in New York all last week. Yes, I can contact Shadow when I have to. Why? She's a client, that's why, and she needs me on the street, not in jail. Once that changes I'll have about as much luck calling her as you will."

"A client? Really. So, what does a freak of nature like that need with a PI?"

"Information. She's looking for someone too."

"Linwood. Son of a bitch, that's what you're doing for her. You're hunting Linwood."

"Actually, it's his boss I'm after, but first I need to get a name to look for. The problem you have right now isn't Linwood, it's the one above him in the chain of command."

"And that's why you're so willing to do me a favor."

"Busted. You're good, Chief. So, are we able to work together here?"

"There's a lot of people dead in this city and you have access to the killer. I should just grab your ass and drag you into the station."

"Go ahead and try, see where it gets you. Look, you came to me, remember. You want the drugs and the violence in this city stopped. I'm telling you, that's going to happen. You want to speed this up, help me find Linwood and his boss. I'll pass along the information to Shadow and she'll clean this mess up. The violence will stop, the drugs will dry up, and you'll get your city back. Your call."

The chief ran his fingers through his iron gray hair. "All right, girl. I'm desperate here. We do this your way."

"So, give already."

"What???"

"I gave you the information you asked for. I want something in return. If you've got the name of Linwood's boss I want it. If you have a location for Linwood, I want it."

"I don't have a location for him, just a phone number."

"I've already got that."

"Then you're as far ahead on that as I am. His boss? I overheard him call someone on the phone Mr. Briggs. Sounded like he was talking to a superior. That's all I have. You're going to tell that to Shadow, aren't you?"

"Damn right I am. That's how I get paid."

"So, what's the deal with the Viper?"

"What? Hold on now, this is a different case we're talking about here."

"Okay, so, what have you got on him?"

"Man's a wild card. Sometimes he runs with Lady Shadow and sometimes he runs alone. If you want more on him go to somebody else. The man's too dangerous and violent. I'm not touching that one."

"Fair enough. I can send my own guys after him once the Linwood thing is out of the way and I can get back to work in my own city. I have to tell you, Miss Elmore, this was a lot easier than I expected."

"I'm not the enemy, Chief, just a cautious P.I."

"I get that. Can I ask you something?"

"Shoot."

"Why did you hire Walsh after he was the one who started this whole war Linwood has going against you?"

"He didn't start it, chief, he was just doing his job. After Lady Shadow tossed him and his partner around he lost all interest in police work. He likes gathering information, but not the rough stuff. It seemed like a good fit."

"I get that. Some guys just aren't cut out for the tough stuff. Can I call you at this number if I get anything more?"

"Sure can."

He pushed his own card across the table to him. "The information flows both ways, right?"

She gazed into his eyes for a moment, then nodded. "Fair enough, Chief. Now, it's time for me to disappear." She arose and walked away.

The chief tossed down the rest of his coffee. It was cold. He dropped too much money on the table and followed her out, but the street was empty. The only other woman he could see was a black woman in a flamboyant dress climbing into a car. He shook his head and returned to the station house.

As Ellen drove away, her passenger morphed back into Seline. "So, how'd I do, boss?"

"You're really getting the hang of this, girl. I'll be out of a job in no time."

"The hell you will, Ellen Cameron. I haven't even started to scratch the surface of what you can teach, besides, you're a great kisser."

"Oh yeah? I'm not so sure about that. I think I need more practice."

Seline laughed with delight. "Oh yeah, want some help with the homework?" Just then her cell phone rang.

"Seline."

"It's Vic. I just spotted Linwood at a coffee shop down on East Fourth." Ellen had overheard. She pulled the car over to the curb and held out her hand for the phone. Seline smiled as she passed it over.

"Vic, it's Ellen. Get your butt out of there right now. East Fourth is no place for a pretty white boy who is averse to violence."

"I wasn't in the cafe, Ellen, just driving by hoping to get lucky and I did. I recognized the guy he was talking to. A local drug dealer named Iggy. I think Shadow and Viper can pick up Iggy and find Linwood from there."

"Sounds good. Return to the office and we'll make plans from there."

"Roger that."

Ellen passed the phone back to Seline and pulled back out into traffic. "Looks like we caught a break," said Seline. "What's out next move?"

"First we shake the tail we picked up back at the cafe, then we go home."

"We're being followed?"

"Big black Caddy, probably feds or friends of Linwood."

"Shit," snarled Seline. "Slow down a bit so I can get a read on these guys." Ellen slowed the car slightly and Seline let her awareness float back to the car half a block behind them. It was the two agents she had manhandled at the condo. "Feds. It's Heckle and Jeckle, the two morons who work for Linwood. You know, the two who rousted us at the condo before I broke cover. How the hell did those two nitwits pick up our trail?"

"Just bad luck," sighed Ellen. "They were probably watching the Chief of Police and recognized me sitting in the car."

"Dammit anyway. Pull over and park; I'll get rid of these guys."

"Seline, what are you going to do?"

"Oh, I won't hurt them, but I'm going to have some fun with these two. Just watch and enjoy." She was grinning wickedly, and Ellen chuckled as she pulled over. Half a block back the big Cadillac pulled over as well.

It was the black woman in the brightly colored dress who got out of Ellen's car. She walked back along the street until she reached the two agents. With a dazzling smile she stepped around to the driver's side and tapped politely on the window. Angrily, the man lowered the window, then screamed as she threw a rattlesnake inside. Both men fled the car, screaming in terror while the woman just continued to smile at them.

"Oh my god, what did you throw into their car?" asked Ellen, as she pulled away, still watching the woman in the dress shouting at the two men.

"Rattlesnake," replied Seline, still tightly focused. Finally she relaxed. "Okay, we're too far away for me to hold the illusion." A grin of pure mischief spread across her face. "Oh man, the look on his face was priceless."

They were still laughing as they reached the mansion and hid the car in the garage. Victor was already there and wanted to know what was so funny. Ellen told him. Vic shook his head and pointed a finger at Seline. "Shadow, you're a mean woman. Good one."

"Thanks," she grinned. "Debbie, we have a name for you to track down while we're waiting for dark."

"What's the name?"

"Mr. Briggs, possibly a CIA agent, possibly Linwood's boss and partner in crime."

"Mr. Briggs. That's all I've got to work with?"

Seline still had that mischievous grin on her face. "Come on, Deb, if it was easy anybody could do it. You're the champ, that's why we bring you the hard stuff."

"Flattery won't get you anywhere, Lady Shadow. Try a raise," quipped Debbie, as she returned to her computer and set to work.

A moment later Debbie noticed a mug of coffee appear at her elbow. "Best I could do," Seline said with a wink.

"Gods, you're awful. Thanks for the coffee." Smiling, Debbie went back to the task at hand.

AS DARKNESS FELL, A steel door rose and the Vipermobile roared out onto the street. A short while later it was parked in the shadows. "That's him," said Vic as he pointed out a seedy looking character. "Do you want to take him off world or can I have him?"

"Keep him alive, at least until we get what we need."

"I'll put him in the trunk, then we can take him down by the bridge to answer a few questions." The Viper's armor appeared on him as he exited the car. A few swift strides set him among the five men gathered around Iggy. Three melted away like mist, two more fell unconscious to the ground. Iggy made no more than six strides before he was caught in a sleeper hold. Viper dragged the unconscious body to the car and dumped it in the trunk.

Everybody had stayed well back. Nobody wanted to go head to head with the Viper. Besides there was a huge cobra riding shotgun in his car. There was a sigh of relief as the car sped away. Linwood was informed before the car disappeared around the block.

Iggy was awake by the time they reached the pillars of the bridge and released him from the trunk. "Where's Linwood?" demanded Viper, as he threw the man hard against a concrete pillar. "Talk! Where do I find Linwood?"

"I dunno, man," stammered the drug dealer.

"Try again," snarled the Viper, as he grabbed the man by the throat and lifted him off the ground.

Choking and gagging, Iggy tried to pry the Viper's fingers away, his feet kicking feebly in the air. "I dunno. Nobody knows where he sleeps, man. The dude don't trust nobody."

Viper dropped him. Iggy sank slowly to the ground, gasping and dragging as much air into his lungs as possible. "Linwood, he don't trust nobody. He finds us when he wants to. Nobody knows where his crib is." He was staring up at that cold impassive mask, trembling. "Please, don't kill me. I can't help you. I'd tell you if I knew."

Suddenly he noticed the woman. Swallowing hard and trying to press himself back inside the concrete pillar, he watched her approach. Oh Christ. Shadow. She's not even human. She reached out with her staff and touched his chest. It burned like hellfire and he shrank away with a hiss of pain. "You know more than you tell," she said in a hollow voice that could not have come from a woman's throat. She dropped the staff which instantly became a live cobra. It fixed its eyes on him and flared its hood with a hiss. "Ask him again."

There was a soft chuckle behind the snake mask as that mountain of armored muscle dragged him to his feet. "Talk to me, Iggy. It's Linwood we want, not you. Where can we find him?"

"Tuesday, there's a shipment coming in Tuesday night. He'll be at the old warehouse."

"Try again. I burned that down."

Iggy began to babble as the cobra slithered closer. "No, man, no. It's underneath. In the basement and sewers. That's where they make up the stuff. That's where we pick up the product. That's how we move it through the city. Linwood will be there. Please, call it off."

The woman hissed and the cobra turn to strike at her. She caught it easily and it was a staff again. "We have what we need, Viper. Kill him or not as you choose."

Iggy wept, begged, and pleaded but the big man in the mask didn't move or speak. Finally he turned aside and got back in the car to race away leaving his victim alone beneath the bridge.

"Will he warn Linwood?" asked Shadow.

"He doesn't dare. If he admits he was taken, that he sang like a bird, Linwood will kill him, and he knows it. No, Iggy will quietly disappear. Linwood will smell a rat and be on full alert, but he won't change his plans. There's too much money at stake and not enough time to change the location. Even if he does, we know there's a big shipment of drugs due into the city this Tuesday. Want to head for the docks and see if we can locate this underground warehouse of theirs?"

"No. There's a chance Linwood won't change his plans. If we start sniffing around he just might. Let's leave it sit for the two days and see if we get lucky. Let's go home."

"Home it is."

The big car raced through the city then disappeared. This time they hid it in the underground garage at the mansion. It was a lucky thing they did. The next day the warehouse was raided by the police. All they found was a snug apartment and an old car.

The Hunt Goes On

Debbie and Victor awakened to the sound of heavy fists pounding on the steel doors below. They hastily pulled on clothes, then Vic went down to see what was going on. Debbie took out an automatic weapon and set herself at the top of the stairs.

"Settle down," Vic bellowed. "Who are you and what the hell do you want?"

"Open up, this is the police. We have a warrant to search these premises."

"Hang on."

Vic waved Debbie back then raised the door. His former partner slapped a warrant against his chest. "What the hell are you doing here, Walsh?"

"I live here. The question is, what the hell are you doing here and what do you expect to find?"

"We got a tip somebody is running a meth lab here. Go ahead and search the place boys. So, who's that at the top of the stairs pointing a gun at the police?"

"That's Debbie and she has a gun because she doesn't know what's going on. Debbie sweetheart, can you put the coffee on for the city's finest here, please. Sorry we don't have any donuts, fellas."

"Very funny, Walsh."

"So, go ahead and look her over while Debbie gets the coffee ready. I promise there's nothing here that'll make you piss your pants."

"Shut the fuck up, Walsh, you frigging coward."

"Me? I'm not the one who pissed himself."

One of the other policemen grinned as he overheard. "What's this about old Jim pissing himself?"

"It was when we went after that P.I. woman. Lady Shadow showed up, she was unhappy, and Jimmy pissed himself. Can't blame him though. That woman is scary as hell." The other policemen were snickering now, and the big man was red faced and angry. "So, who told you we had a meth lab?"

"None of your fucking business, asshole," snarled Victor's former partner.

"Right. So, you satisfied guys?" Vic asked the other men.

"Nothing here but a bunch of furniture and packing boxes. Nice little apartment though, Vic. Good coffee, too."

"Screw that, what's through that door?" said the big cop.

"Isn't locked, take a look."

One of the men opened the door and looked inside. "Nothing there but Vic's old car," he said.

"So tell me, Jim, when did you go on the take? Is that new, or were you always dirty?"

"Just what are you trying to imply?" asked the big cop as he stepped close to go nose to nose with Victor.

Vic didn't back down. "You got a tip. That fed, Linwood, has a hate on for the woman I work for. Damn funny how easy you found me down here. I'd say your fed buddy is on a fishing expedition. Tell that asshole I just work for the woman and I'm not working anything related to him at all. He's fishing in the wrong waters. I don't keep any files here or anything else pertaining to my job. This is my home. I don't bring my work home."

"You never did; that's why you were such a shitty cop."

"Yeah, well, I like my new job. I get paid better, I don't have to face the same dangers every day, and I don't have to listen to you all day."

"Sounds like a triple crown win to me," laughed one of the other policemen. "Come on, guys, there's nothing here. Sorry we busted in on you, Vic. Thanks for the coffee, ma'am." He waved at Debbie then led the others out to their van. Vic's former partner was the last to go and he glared at Vic threateningly on the way out.

"I don't think he likes you," said Debbie, as she put her arms around him from behind.

Victor gently squeezed the hands that held him. "That man will never know how many times I wanted to kick his sorry ass over the past three years. He got a tip? The hell he did. Linwood sent him. He'd have come while we were gone, but he wouldn't be able to break in through those doors, so he tried to surprise us early."

"Any idea what he was really looking for?"

"The Vipermobile, I imagine." Vic sighed and turned in her arms to kiss her lightly. "Hi, pretty lady. Is there any of that coffee left or did those greedy cops drink it all?"

"Come on, handsome," she said, taking his hand and leading him back up the stairs. "I'll make you a new pot."

A few moments later Vic sat enjoying a mug of fresh coffee and watching Debbie dance around the kitchen preparing breakfast. She felt the eyes on her and turned to face him, beaming a bright smile. "What's on your mind, big fella?"

"You are, pretty lady."

"Nice try, champ, but I can see you're bugged about something. What's going through that head of yours?" She set breakfast on the table then sat facing him, arching an eyebrow to encourage him to speak.

Vic sighed and studied his hands for a moment then looked up. "Deb, I wanted to do this another way, something a lot more romantic. However, events are not going to allow me the leisure."

"Why, Victor Walsh, are you trying to propose to me?" She gave him a wicked grin and he popped up his armor. "Hey, why the hell did you put on the armor?"

"So you can't see how red my face is."

"You take that off right now and look me in the eye."

The armor vanished and he met her eyes. "Yes, you savage tease, I'm trying to propose to you."

"So do it then." She was still grinning wickedly, and he was blushing furiously.

Vic chuckled and shook his head. He met her gaze again and spoke. "Debbie, honey, will you marry me?"

"Oh my god, you're serious aren't you?"

"Yes I am, so say yes or shoot me now, because ..."

He got no further as she laid a finger across his lips. "Vic, this is a crazy and dangerous world. If I have to face it I want to face it with you. Yes, I'll marry you, anytime, anywhere."

He gripped her hands tightly, the relief sweeping across his face and the joy returning. She felt bad about teasing him, but she really hadn't allowed herself to hope. He pulled her toward him and kissed her softly. "Live with me until we pick a time and do the deed?"

"Sure. Vic Honey, what else is on your mind?"

"They came at us today. That tells me Linwood is going after anyone close to Seline. He's figured out who she is, suspects I'm Viper, and I don't think your place is any safer than here."

"Yeah, you could be right about that. You're thinking we should take Ellen up on her offer of that super gorgeous apartment in her mansion?"

"Yeah. I know it's pretty luxurious, but you're tough. You could get used to it."

"In a heartbeat," she grinned. "Can we keep the country house? You know, in case we want to get away once in a while."

"Absolutely, but not until after this thing with Linwood is over. That bastard is making me paranoid."

"Yeah, well, like Seline says, even paranoids have enemies. Come on, let's get dressed and go tell them the news."

"First things first," he said. He went to a cupboard and pulled out a small box. Grinning with delight, he slipped the ring on her finger.

THERE WERE SQUEALS of delight from the girls, and much blushing from Vic, then they got down to business. "I want to be there when you move," said Seline.

"All assistance gratefully accepted," said Victor.

"Not for the lifting, big guy, I want to keep an eye on the neighborhood. We can get the guys with the unmarked truck to do the heavy lifting. I plan to make sure there are no prying eyes in the area. Maybe I'll get lucky and Linwood himself will show up."

"I doubt we'll get that lucky," said Ellen, "but I wouldn't be surprised to see those two goons of his show up."

"They'll be sorry if they do. I'm getting tired of this whole thing."

"Easy, sweetie, they're just the hired hands here. Linwood is the one you want," said Ellen.

"I know, but they're standing between me and my prey. They're an irritant and will be removed." She had shifted into full Shadow mode, pacing about the room. The dragon had also appeared and was watching her carefully. "I will be vigilant. Any who seek to spy upon us will regret their decision."

"You need to eat something, Shadow," said Ellen. "You're getting cranky. Come, let's go explore the kitchen while these two love birds make their arrangements."

Slowly Seline returned to herself. "Sorry, guys. I guess I'm just getting impatient to get this done. The longer it takes the closer he seems to get to us. I don't like that."

"Maybe that's not a bad idea," said Ellen. "Why don't we choose the playing field for once."

"You mean, set a trap for him?" asked Seline.

"Well, yes, in a manner of speaking. Let them see Victor and Debbie packing up, but when the truck leaves, you and I lead them someplace completely different. When Linwood comes at us we'll be waiting. Rather, you'll be waiting, waiting to take him off world."

Seline nodded. "I like it. Woman, you have the best ideas. Especially the one about the kitchen."

"Yes, my darling, come with me and I'll feed you. That'll make it all better." She took Seline by the hand and led her to the kitchen. Victor grinned and stole a kiss as they left. Debbie picked up her phone and began to make the arrangements for their move.

A STREET WOMAN SITTING against the warehouse wall seemed to be asleep. She ignored the people going in and out carrying boxes and household effects. Finally she roused herself and shouted. "Hey, what's going on? You people got anything to eat? Any spare change?" A hand reached out to escort her inside as a voice replied to her query.

"Come on in, there's plenty of food and we can't take it with us. Help yourself."

Inside the warehouse Ellen brought the woman some food and water. "Gods I love how you always feed me."

"All my pleasure," smiled Ellen. "Any signs of spies?"

"Yep, the gruesome twosome are in a brown Ford just around the block. One is actually using a periscope to peer around the corner."

"Really? Oh my, how inconspicuous."

"Yeah. I wonder who they get to tie their shoes for them in the morning. Geez. So, have you got a place picked out for them?"

"Yes. There's an old house not far from the building Linwood burned down. He probably knows that you know where his operation is working from. By making them think Vic is moving in to keep an eye on him will make him believe it. He'll move on you there, no doubt about it."

"Truck's loaded," called a voice.

"Pick me up around the block," said Seline as she rose and headed for the door, still in the old street woman disguise. Once outside she hobbled around the corner then morphed back into herself. A moment later Ellen picked her up.

They followed the truck for three blocks, the two agents following at a distance. Seline began to focus while Ellen drove. A fog bank slowly appeared, and the agents had to get closer to keep their quarry in sight. A long drive through the city and they saw the truck pull up at an old empty building. They knew where they were. Chuckling with delight they watched until the men began to unload the truck. After a few moments they drove away to report to Linwood.

"Looks like they bought it," said Seline, as she watched with her special sight. "They're gone." She let the illusion of the truck fade, then Ellen drove home by a circuitous route, just in case. Seline was almost asleep in her seat. Holding the illusion for that long had drained her.

"Aw, my poor Seline. You'd better have a nap this afternoon. You want to be on top of your game when Linwood shows up tonight." Her only answer was a soft murmur as Seline snuggled deeper into the seat.

They arrived back at the mansion. Ellen tucked Seline into bed for a nap while the men unloaded the truck into the south wing. It was nearly dark when Seline reappeared, ready for battle. "Are you so sure he'll come tonight?" asked Vic, as they headed downstairs to the hidden garage and the waiting Viper. "I'm sure," she replied as she climbed inside and he started the engine. The big car roared to life then Seline hit the button to raise the door. "Tomorrow's Tuesday; his shipment will be arriving. He has to finish us off tonight."

Vic nodded and brought up his armor as the huge car sped through the gathering dusk. Seline had already morphed into Lady Shadow. She mentally hardened her own armor; She didn't trust Linwood. He had been far too resourceful before. Lady Shadow wasn't taking any chances.

Three blocks from the house he stopped the car, and they went ahead on foot. Nearing the house, they faded into the shadows. Seline concentrated and caught hushed conversations. "They're here."

"Wish I could hear like you do."

She grasped his arm and he, too, heard the voices. "No, Linwood, this is stupid, man."

"Just shut up and do as you're told."

"Oh hell no. Look, you ran with Ronaldo and got his gang killed. All of them dead. Then you went to Jazz, and Viper cleaned him out. You went after that woman and got more guys killed. Now you come to us, the last resort, the guys you wouldn't spit on a year ago. Well this gang is about keeping each other alive. We'll move product for you, no problem. Go up against the Viper? No fucking way. You're on your own with this one."

They heard the click of a gun being cocked. "That wasn't a request from the pope, asshole, it was an order from the man with a gun to your head. He's got to be in there. One man and one woman. You go in, kill the man, and the woman is yours, plus I keep the cops off you forever. The city is yours."

"I don't want the man's woman. That was Ronaldo's thing, man. He was one super sick bastard. No, we don't fight your battles, we move your product, and you pay in money, hard cash, not women and children, you sick fuck."

"You do as you're told, Ricky, or I shoot you right here, right now."

"Bad idea, Linwood. See my guys? They're holding guns on you too. I go out, you go out. So here's the deal. You want this man dead, you're coming in with us. Oh, does that scare you? Now who's the pussy?"

"Fine," snarled Linwood. "Let's go then, super hero."

"Inside or out here?" asked Viper, as Shadow released his arm and the voices fell silent.

"Inside," she replied. "We don't want them escaping, especially Linwood. Come."

There was a crash as the door to the old house was kicked in. Several men rushed in, spraying bullets at random. They found nothing. They quickly spread through the house looking for their intended victims. Suddenly all hell broke out behind them.

The Viper came in from behind, his guns blazing. Several men fell and others fled. Those upstairs screamed and tried to flee, but Lady Shadow was on the stairs, her daggers flashing. More men fell. She saw Linwood duck into a bedroom but couldn't go after him. Two others attacked her from the side. Terrified when their bullets seemed to have no effect on her, they tried to flee, but she cut them down.

Viper was on the stairs now, his guns silent. His blades were all he wanted now, but there was no one to fight. He reached the top to see Shadow finish off the last man, then kick in a door and leap inside. There was the sound of shattering glass, then Shadow swearing profusely.

Linwood had no illusion about his chances. Those stupid gangsters would never be able to stop her. Just as she kicked open the door, he threw himself through the window. He was lucky, he landed heavily on a part of the first floor roof then rolled off and fell to the ground. He gasped in pain, but fought his way to his feet. A car skidded to a halt, and he practically fell into it as it sped away with screeching tires.

"Dirty, rotten, egg-sucking son of a bitch, he slipped through my fingers again," snarled Shadow. "Aeroth!" The dragon appeared outside the broken window, and she leaped through to its back. With a scream of challenge the beast leaped into the air and followed the direction the car had taken.

Viper turned back, looking for survivors. He found a couple, but they were badly wounded. He dragged then down out of the house and dropped them on the sidewalk. They cowered in fear as the huge armored man in the snake mask stared at then silently. "Please, man, I'm bleeding bad here..."

"Shut up. Next time you idiots want to play in the big leagues, don't." With that, he turned and strode away. A few moments later they heard the roar of the engine and the scream of tires as the big car sped away. Shaking badly, one man phoned for an ambulance.

The viper came speeding up the driveway just in time for Victor to see the dragon land by the door. The door flew open as the car screeched to a stop and Seline slid slowly from the back of the beast. She was bleeding and barely conscious. Victor scooped her up and carried her inside. "We lost him, Vic," Seline said in a barely audible voice.

"Hush now, we have to get you an ambulance," said Ellen.

"No, no, Ellen, no. Vic, put me on the couch. Ellen, here, hold your hand over the wound." Seline took a ragged breath then called. "Moragah?" Ellen felt the vast loving presence of the goddess surround them.

"I am here, my priestess. You are wounded. Ellen, hold her gently and hold her in your mind as she is whole and sound. I will heal her injuries." Ellen closed her eyes and pictured Seline laughing and teasing her. Suddenly she felt something in her hand. It was the bullet that had been lodged in her back.

"She is resting now. When she awakens she will be fully healed and restored. I am well pleased with you Ellen, you and Seline." Moragah sent another wave of loving, healing energy through them both

then withdrew.

"Wow," said Victor, "that was amazing."

"You can say that again," agreed Debbie.

"Wow, that was amazing."

Ellen sighed and cuddled Seline closer. "What happened, Vic?"

"They were there, Linwood and the last of the gangs in the city. The gang didn't want any part of it, but Linwood forced the deal. They charged into the house and we went in after them. It was pretty crazy for a while, bullets flying everywhere. My armor held up and Seline had hardened hers as well. She cornered Linwood upstairs, but he went out through a window. Shadow called the dragon and went after him. Apparently, the damn snake slithered away again."

"Yeah, he did." Seline groaned as she sat up and stretched, then reached over to kiss Ellen softly. "Thank you, my darling."

"For what?"

"For being you. For loving me." She stood up and began to move through a series of light exercises to test her flexibility and range of motion. "Good as new," she said, as she began pacing about the room. "I have no idea where they took him, but Aeroth and I found no trace of him. I wanted to keep looking for him, but Aeroth said no and brought me home."

"Then I owe you, most beautiful of beasts," smiled Ellen, as she approached the dragon which had followed them inside. She hugged it around the neck and it nuzzled her fondly. "One day you will have to tell me how you get through those small doors."

"Dragon magic," came a soft voice in her mind. Her eyes opened wide in surprise and the beast winked at her.

Seline was still pacing. "Dammit, this is getting irritating. I almost had him. No matter," she said as she morphed into Shadow, "tomorrow night will see the end of him."

"What do you mean?" asked Ellen.

"The drug shipment is arriving tomorrow night. He'll be there to receive it and make payment. He's injured, and doesn't have access to healing as I have, but he will be there."

"We need to make some changes," said Ellen.

Lady Shadow stopped pacing and faced her. "Please forgive me, Ellen. You're our greatest asset and I've ignored that in a misguided attempt to keep you safe. What do you suggest we do?"

"Stop pacing and let me think." She smiled and kissed Shadow on the cheek. Shadow sat and Ellen began the pacing. Finally she stopped and sighed. "All right, Lady Shadow, is the armor you wear the only armor you can make real?"

"No. This form is how I am most comfortable; this is how I feel myself to be."

"It's inadequate. You're fighting modern weapons with medieval armor. You need to reach out into the future for your armor and weapons. This is the first step."

Lady Shadow stood and closed her eyes. Her armor shimmered into some sort of flexible metal that glowed softly and conformed to her body, drawing a soft whistle from Vic. Debbie slapped his shoulder. Shadow opened her eyes. "Viper, your weapon of choice?"

"Glock 22, why?"

"That is what you wear?"

"Yes. Do you have armor piercing rounds?"

"Yes, why?"

"Shoot me."

"What??? Now ..."

"Do it!"

He nodded slowly and drew his gun. "Ready?"

"Do it." He fired and the bullet appeared less than an inch from her chest then fell to the floor. "Again, the full load." He fired until the gun was empty. The bullets lay on the floor at her feet. She looked at them and nodded in satisfaction. Her familiar cloak appeared over the new armor, and she smiled. "Be still, Viper." She focused for a moment then his armor changed as well. He still had the black with snakes coiling over it and the mask, but now it too had a soft glow.

Lady Shadow nodded her approval, then turned to Ellen. "Accomplished. What's next?"

"Had you not been shot, could you have caught him?" asked Ellen.

"Yes. The shock of the bullet hitting me staggered me for a moment and that allowed his escape."

"Good, so now we have that angle covered. Now tell me about the terrain you will face tonight."

"Vic, you're up." Shadow had morphed back into Seline.

He let his armor disappear, then sat. "Well, it's in a basement; under the building where he bombed us and burned it down. Apparently the basement survived. They get the shipments through there and distribute the drugs through the city via the sewer system. That building was near the dock so I'm guessing they'll have plenty of fire power there to guard it while it's transported into that basement."

"They'll be expecting you to hit them above ground," mused Ellen. "I think your chances are a lot better if you go in through the sewers and take them when they think they're safe. Also, they'll be unpacking and repackaging the shipment for distribution so there will fewer gunmen on full alert. Add to that the new armor and I believe our chances are much better."

Seline leaped to her feet. "Our chances? Just what do you mean by, *our*?

"I'm going with you. I'll need armor, too."

"You aren't going anywhere, my darling woman. You're the brains of the outfit, yes. And I admit your talents have been underutilized but ..."

"Whoa, easy there, my warrior princess. I'm not trying to get in the way, I just want to be close in case that bastard tries to slip away again. If I had been outside tonight ..."

"You'd have been shot or worse by the two goons out there. Ellen, please reconsider this. We need you in one piece and I'm not going to be able to focus if I know you might be in harm's way."

"All right, I'll reconsider under one condition."

"Name your terms, sexy woman." Seline was grinning now.

"When you work alone, you use illusion to great effect. When you work with Viper, you go in with the same style he uses. That's how you keep getting hurt, you abandon illusion for brute force. Okay, so you're a lot stronger than Vic, but that's not your natural style and it isn't working for you. Use illusion. Sneak up on these guys, send them someplace they don't want to be, introduce them to a whole world of crazy, then and only then, take them down."

Seline stepped closer and gently pulled Ellen into her arms. "Oh gods, Ellen, I'm so sorry."

"Whatever for, sweetie?"

"For not consulting you more. I'm beginning to see my weaknesses and your strengths fill that void so perfectly. Yes, my darling, you're absolutely right. That's how we'll do it. I can just imagine their faces as Viper comes walking out of a burning mist, a cobra on each shoulder while a dozen of me comes at them from the walls and ceiling. Oh yeah, this is going to be fun."

"Now you're getting the idea," grinned Ellen. "That vivid imagination of yours is your greatest weapon. Use it, girl. Use it and drive them crazy."

Below the City

"Where are you going?" asked Ellen. After their planning session, Seline slept for several hours then arose and dressed for the streets.

"I'm going to do a bit of recon," she replied. "I'm going to take a page from Lady Justice and slip down into the sewer tunnels. I want to see the lay of the land before Vic and I go in tonight. Don't worry, I'll be careful; no one will see me, I promise."

"Here, study this first," said Debbie, as she took Seline by the arm and led her into the office. Vic was there studying a strange map on the desk. "It's a map of the storm sewers."

"This looks like our entry point," said Vic, as he tapped the map with his finger.

Seline glanced at the map. "This one looks a lot closer," she said, indicating a different entry point.

"They'll be using that one, and probably watching it. I'd rather be behind them."

"Second that. You really think they're watching it now?"

"I would be."

Seline sighed and let her shoulders slump. "Yeah, I would too. Okay, no scouting mission."

"It would be different on the street," said Ellen. "You could use various disguises and get a close look, but what could you use for a disguise down there?"

"You'd be surprised."

"Ewww," said Debbie. "I don't even want to know."

"I can think of a better use of our time," said Ellen. "You're going to take these guys off world, throw them into something nasty. Vic will be trying to function in all of that. I'm sure he'd be happier if he could tell what was going on."

"That's why you always go hardcore and avoid the illusions when I'm with you," said Vic. "You don't want to mess me up."

"Busted," sighed Seline.

"Ellen's right, that's just getting you hurt. Stay home today, show me what I'm in for tonight so I can be useful."

"All right, big fella, but remember, you asked for it." Suddenly Vic was in another world, a world of darkness and ruin. Strange creatures slunk around, sniffing at dead bodies. Suddenly an armored man twice his size leaped at him swinging a huge sword at his neck. Vic swallowed hard but remained still. Another creature stuck a shield out to defend him, but the sword shattered it. The two creatures moved away, locked in a battle to the death.

"I can see through it, Seline. I mean it's transparent, I can see right through it."

"I know, I won't make it real to you now, but tonight it'll be real. You have to ignore what's happening around you. Stay focused on the target. Linwood."

"Gotcha."

"Now, here's something else I want to throw at them." Suddenly there were snakes everywhere, crawling in masses on the ground, up his legs, and then the dragons came. Through the madness a warrior ran, ignoring or dodging the battles and creatures in her way. It was Shadow, but Shadow as he had not known her. Shadow, spattered in blood, her lip peeled back in a snarl, and cold death in her eyes. Vic shivered as he looked in those eyes. And then it all vanished.

He allowed the armor to vanish then shook off the spell. "Wow, that's taking the game up a level."

"She has to, Vic, we all do," said Ellen. "These guys are trained, professional killers and spies. Either we play at their level, or we get obliterated. Fighting the lower level guys we did fine, but Linwood is obviously in a different league. Shadow has to up her game to match him and whoever she goes up against in the future. So do you."

"So, better armor and stronger weapons?"

"And smarter tactics," said Shadow. "We've underestimated this man, and we can do so no longer. Ellen, you must play a larger role in the planning."

"I will. I've been holding back a bit. I guess I thought that, with everything you guys can do, you didn't really need me."

Seline morphed back. "Honey ..."

"I know, I know, but that was then. I can clearly see now, you two savages need a guiding hand. You both have so much to learn." She was grinning and they both began to laugh.

DEBBIE'S OLD CAR STOPPED and two figures got out. "Thanks for the lift, lady." To anyone watching they were two teenagers. They leaned against a building until the girl spoke. "Clear." She morphed into Shadow, complete with new armor. The updated version of Viper stood beside her. "Ready?"

"Ready," he replied, as he bent and lifted the manhole cover off. She dropped easily through the hole and he followed.

The cobra headed staff appeared in her hand, its glowing eyes giving them enough light to see their way. They had not gone far when Viper sensed something behind him. He stopped still. Something moved, something huge and scaled moved closer. "Aeroth, is that you?" he asked softly. The dragon snorted and nudged him forward. "Dang dragon, you scared the crap out of me." The dragon snorted and nudged him again. "It's not funny, damn it." Another snort and a giggle from Shadow.

"Stop it, both of you. This is serious business," she said, trying to sound stern.

A moment later the light went out. "They're up ahead," she whispered. They moved closer and saw men bringing large bales of something from a boat that rocked slightly in the sewage outfall. They were cursing about the stink.

One of the new special agents was directing the task. "Just stop whining and get those bales up the ladder." It was a steep climb, but doable. They continued to grumble but did as they were told.

"Wait until they get it all ashore," whispered Shadow. Viper nodded and they waited, and watched. They could hear more people working in the building above.

"Maybe we should have gone at them from the street," whispered Vic.

"Maybe I should have scouted the damned territory," she grumbled. "Too late now. They're done." The men climbed back in their boat and pushed off, silently paddling their way out into the harbor.

"What the hell are you doing?" asked Viper.

"Sending a text."

"What? Now?"

"Oh yeah. It shouldn't be long now. Just be patient."

"Shadow, what did you do?"

"I texted the chief of police. Told him a big shipment of drugs just landed and where to find them. He'll jump all over it and that'll force those guys all down here where we want them."

"I love it," chuckled Viper, slipping his weapons into his gloved hands. This new armor was lighter and more flexible than the old leather. He grinned in anticipation.

It seemed like a long wait, but it wasn't. Suddenly there was a panic up the ladder and bales of drugs began falling down followed by several men. A bullhorn could be heard outside. "Attention, you men in the basement of the burned out building. This is the police. You're surrounded. Come out with your hands in the air and no one gets hurt. You have ten seconds to comply."

The last of the drugs hit the damp floor and three more men followed. Linwood was the last. He flipped a switch in his hand and the room above exploded. He turned to his men. "Get those ..." Linwood wasn't where he expected to be. Instead of a storm sewer he was in a bombed out city. Broken buildings and rubble were everywhere. He knew instantly who he was dealing with. "It's Shadow, find her, kill her," he shouted at his confused and frightened men. "This is all an illusion. Find the bitch." To emphasize his point he lashed out with a boot, expecting his foot to pass right through the broken concrete at his feet. Instead he hit something solid with a painful jar.

"Fuck!" He danced about for a moment then the snakes came. He and his men fought them. Suddenly the snakes were gone and a small group of savage warriors were there. The sounds of gunfire filled the air along with the screams of the wounded. Bullets hit friend and foe alike, but the aliens kept coming. Swords bit into unprotected flesh.

Linwood saw Shadow and Viper amid the aliens, and he slunk away, staying low, moving in the direction he hoped would take him out of the illusion. He knew he had it right when he felt the water on his feet even thought all he could see was dirt and broken concrete. Normally he would have gone at her, but he'd been hurt in the attack on the old house. His grin of delight faded as he sensed something close by. It was Viper.

"Don't go yet, Linwood. The party's just getting started." Linwood fired until both his guns were empty, but Viper just shrugged it off. "That the best you've got?"

Linwood started to sweat. A glance told him the illusion was gone, his men were down, and Shadow was coming for him. He leaped at Viper, going for a groin shot. Viper blocked it easily. Linwood was a well-trained killer with years of field experience, but he'd never faced a man like this before. The Viper's martial arts were equal to his own and the man was wearing some sort of armor. He was big, strong, and the armor didn't slow him down at all. Viper was toying with him.

"Enough of this," said Shadow, as she stepped in, grabbed Linwood, and slammed him against the concrete wall, holding him off his feet with one hand. "Who is your boss?"

That was the last thing Linwood had expected to hear. "What???"

"Who is your boss? Who in the CIA do you answer to?"

"Why do you want to know that? I know you're going to kill me so I'm not telling you anything."

"I'm not after you, moron," said Shadow. "I never was. You started this yourself. I couldn't care less about you. I want the man you answer to. You see, it began with this woman." She waved her hand and Lexa Condon, complete with scar on her head, stood beside her. "She was killed and disposed of. I slew her killer then began to follow the trail to find the man ultimately responsible."

"What was so damn special about her?"

"She was my lover and I will avenge her. Now tell me who you answer to, who gave that order. Tell me the truth and I won't kill you. Lie to me and I will."

"Briggs. Eamon Briggs. He's my boss. He's the one I answer to." She dropped him and he pressed himself tightly to the wall to keep from falling.

"Where do I find this Briggs?"

"West Eighteenth. There's a small travel agency there. He works there."

Shadow turned and walked away. "I have what I need. He's all yours, Viper."

Startled, Linwood locked his eyes on Viper. "Yeah, I was the one after you, dumbass," said Viper. "I hate street gangs. You just keep bringing them in, making them rich on the misery of the innocent." His Glock barked twice and Linwood fell, his career of violence and misery ended at last.

Viper found Shadow waiting for him at the entry point. "The police have found their way in," she said. "They've found the drugs and the bodies. The chief will be happy he has his city back."

"He will. I'm a bit surprised you didn't finish Linwood yourself."

"I said I wouldn't if he talked."

"I'm curious, what would you have done if I'd let him live?"

"Kicked your ass and sent Aeroth to do it."

Viper just chuckled. "Let's get out of here. The cops are all over the place now."

For an answer, Shadow ignored the ladder and leaped. She caught the edge of the manhole and pulled herself through. Viper was close behind. As they reached the street, a car came to life and approached them. They dropped the armor and climbed inside. "Everything go okay?" asked Ellen.

"The new armor worked perfect, the drugs are in the hands of the cops," Seline replied, "and Linwood is dead. Before he departed this world he did give up his boss, Mr. Briggs. The bugger works at a travel agency here in the city."

"Good. That'll give Debbie more to work with. Do you think he's the last one?"

"Hope so. What do you think?"

"I think he is," mused Ellen, as she turned into the long driveway. "With Linwood and someone else skimming off millions, it would have to be the man in charge of the operation. Otherwise, they'd have eliminated Linwood themselves."

"Then, once Debbie has a home address for me, I'll look him up." Seline's voice was sleepy, and she was snuggled into the seat.

Ellen raised the garage door and put the car inside. She turned off the motor as the door closed behind them. "So, Miss Sleepyhead, can you manage or do you want Vic to carry you in again."

"I'll walk. Debbie will beat me up if Vic keeps carrying me around."

"Naw, it'll be me who gets the beating," chuckled Vic.

AS USUAL, SELINE WAS the last one to arrive in the office. She wished everyone a good morning, poured up a giant mug of coffee, then sat to her desk. They waited until she had taken a long sip of her coffee before speaking. Vic went first. "Hey Shadow, you want the good news or the bad first?"

"Couldn't let me have a full coffee first, could you?" she said, shaking a finger at him. "Okay, give me the bad."

"The police found everything last night, except two of the bodies."

"What???

"Yeah, two of the bodies were missing. One was Linwood."

"You're kidding. He got away again?"

"Not unless he's a cat with nine lives. I personally put two rounds in his heart. No way he walked away from that."

"Well, shit," she muttered, unconsciously morphing into Lady Shadow.

"This is a mystery, yes, but is it important to us?" asked Ellen. "Do we care about this right now?"

"No, we don't," replied Shadow, rising to pace about the room.

Ellen caught her arm. "Sit and have your coffee, dear. Debbie has good news."

Just then Debbie's computer made a pinging noise. She turned to the screen. "Oh shit."

"What is it?" asked Shadow.

"I have a home address and a work address for Eamon Briggs," replied Debbie. "However, he's just booked himself on a flight to Tangiers for late this afternoon."

"Aw, crap," said Victor. "He's blowing town. Ah well, no rest for the wicked."

"He'll be at home packing," said Shadow. She drained the last of her coffee and slowly brought herself back to Seline. "Take a breather, Vic.

Spend some time with your woman. Ellen, honey, you want to sit in on this one?"

"Love to, but we'd better get a move on." She headed for the garage with Seline close behind.

"You've got the home address?" asked Seline, as she fastened her seat belt.

"I do indeed." The garage door opened and she sped down the driveway. Once on the street she pushed the speed limit a bit. "How do you want to handle this?"

"We bust into his place, catch him packing, make sure he is the top guy, then finish it."

"And if he isn't the top guy?"

"We get a name and the hunt goes on."

"I want to come in with you."

"Works for me, just get behind me if he starts shooting."

"Count on it, sweet sister."

They arrived to find a car still in the driveway. Grinning, Seline approached the door. It was locked. Ellen grinned and took out her gun as Seline knelt and worked her magic on the lock. It gave way with a soft click. She opened the door cautiously and slipped inside, Ellen right on her heels. They could hear movement upstairs in one of the rooms. They started up but were only halfway there when a tread gave a loud squeak.

A short balding man appeared instantly, a gun in his hand. "What the ..." He got no further as Ellen fired a single shot. He dropped his gun and grabbed his shoulder. He turned to run, but Seline was on him, throwing him into the room where he'd been packing.

"Going somewhere, Eamon?" asked Ellen. "If you want to get there in one piece you'd be well advised to answer a few questions."

"What do you want?"

"Information," replied Seline. "I ..."

Suddenly he dove for the bed and the extra gun he had hidden there. Instead he landed on dirt. Cold, hard, freezing dirt. Startled, he scrambled around for a moment then looked up. He was on a hillside somewhere in a mountain range. It was cold, so cold, and the wind cut through his sweat-stained shirt like a knife. He climbed to his feet, shivering, and backed away from the two women who stood watching him.

"I know who you are," he said through chattering teeth. "This is all illusion. It's not real."

"Funny, your friend Linwood thought the same thing," said Lady Shadow, who was now clothed in her favorite leather armor, a long woolen cloak across her shoulders. The woman with the gun was clothed all in furs with a cloak of finest ermine. Smiling, she put the gun away and pulled on her fur mittens.

Lady Shadow reached out with her staff and poked him in the chest. It burned and he pulled away, hissing in pain. He was now backed against a huge boulder. He shrank against the cold stone as a wolf howled nearby. "They smell the blood from your wound," she said. "I believe they're hungry. So, are you ready to answer a few questions yet?"

"It's all just an illusion," he said.

"Fine, we'll just leave you here then. Aeroth!" To his horror something huge moved the shadows of the dying day. He watched with wide eyes as the dragon approached the women who then mounted its back. Gathering itself it suddenly leaped into the air and spread its massive wings. "Good luck with the wolves," she called as the beast began to rise higher into the air.

That's where he snapped. "Wait! Please. Wait. I'll talk." The dragon banked and settled back to earth.

The two women slid from its back and approached him. "You're Eamon Briggs, supervisor, and fellow thief, to Agent Linwood, deceased, yes?" asked Shadow.

"Yes."

"Are you the man who masterminded the drug smuggling operation into this country?"

"No."

The dragon snorted fire and stepped towards him. "Don't lie to me, he doesn't like it and he can always tell. Try again."

"Yes. I had orders to find a way to fund certain activities. The Agency is under a lot of scrutiny in regards to funding. We dare not use conventional funds. We had to find another way."

"And this was the way you chose?"

"Yes. The director gave me the assignment and he didn't want to know anything about it, he just wanted it done. I made a few connections with para military contractors overseas and we set this up. Please don't kill me. Please."

"Why should I not?" demanded Shadow, but before he could reply, the other whispered in her ear. Lady Shadow nodded then brought her gaze back to the man cowering against the cold, hard stone. "Another possible option has been suggested."

"Anything. I swear it, anything at all."

"Tell him," she said, then turned away to pet the dragon.

The woman in the furs stepped closer. "We will return you to your home. You will not leave the country. Instead you will go to the chief of police and confess in full to the whole operation. Do this and we have no quarrel with you. Fail us and I'll shoot you dead the next time, that is, if Shadow doesn't feed you to the dragon first. So, are we agreed?"

"Yes, yes, I'll do it," he sobbed. Suddenly he felt the warm air. He was back in his bedroom, alone.

"An illusion after all," he muttered, and then he noticed the sleeve of his shirt where the dragon's breath had singed it. He touched it then brought his hand up to his wounded shoulder. With a deep sigh of resignation, he groped for and found his phone. "Hello, police station? Put me through to the chief please. It's CIA Agent Briggs calling."

Outside an old car pulled away from the curb and drove away. "We're good," smiled Seline, as she let her focus return to the car. "He made the call."

The End

AND, JUST FOR FUN, here's the first chapter of the next book in the Children of the Goddess Series. Enjoy!

Lady Seeker
Prudence MacLeod

Finding a Seeker

Lenora Schmidt stood in the driveway staring at the house, dreading going in. This house had been her home for twenty years, but she knew it would be no longer. Not after she delivered the news to her father. She sighed deeply, fighting her desire to run and warring with herself inside.

"He's going to blow his top, you know that," she told herself. "He's going to go batshit crazy and somebody will pay the price, probably me. I'll be lucky if he doesn't kill me outright. Okay, stay sharp, keep a clear path to the door, and face the music. He's going to blame you for this and you know it."

Her father was a violent man, always had been, given over to fits of temper. He'd managed to stay out of prison only because mostly he took out his rage on his wife and children, primarily Lenora. She, on the other hand, had spent much of her young life learning how to duck, lie, hide, and whatever else it took to avoid the beatings. This time she knew there was no way out for her except to run and that would leave her mother to take the beating. She squared her shoulders and stepped through the door.

"Lenora, you're back," exclaimed her mother. "Wilson, she's back."

"You've been gone for weeks," said a heavy set man in his mid forties. "Did you find Belinda?" Belinda was Lenora's younger sister, the apple of her father's eye, and she's been missing for months.

"Yes," Lenora replied softly, staying close to the door. "I found her."

"Well, where is she? Did you bring her home?"

"No, she refused to come."

"Where is she then. I'll go get her myself." He was already getting angry and moving closer to Lenora.

"She's in Los Angeles, but I promised not to tell where."

"What? Just what the hell is going on, young lady? You tell me where your sister is right now." He grabbed Lenora by the front of her jacket, but she squirmed out of it and fell back onto the floor. "Why the hell won't you tell me where she is?" He threw her jacket at her.

Lenora snapped at last. "Because she begged me not to, that's why. You want to know where she is, what she's doing since she ran away from home? She a porn queen."

"What?" That made him pause.

"You heard me, she's a porn queen. She ran away from home, met up with a guy who was nice to her, and he got her into the movies. She actually enjoys her work."

"You're lying, you fucking little bitch. You were always jealous of her. Now tell me the truth." He kicked her hard in the stomach, driving the air from her lungs.

Lenora fought the air back into her body then hurled a movie case like a frisbee. It hit him in the chest. "Look for yourself," she said, as she struggled to her feet.

"Oh sweet Jesus. Oh dear god." He was staring at the cover on the case and the picture of his baby girl, naked with a penis in her mouth. Lenora made a break for the door, but he grabbed her by the hair and hauled her back. "This is all your goddamned fault," he shouted, as he hit her hard. "You were supposed to look after her, keep her out of trouble. Now look what you've done. You've ruined her."

He kept shouting as he kept punching her. Finally he threw her out into the driveway. "You get the fuck outta my sight, you little whore. Don't you dare ever come back here."

Lenora tried to crawl away. She had a broken arm, three loose teeth, two broken ribs, a fractured cheekbone, broken nose, and both her eyes were closed over. Blood oozed from her broken nose as she tried to crawl away, the sounds of her mother's screams ringing in her ears. She almost made it to her car before her reserves ran out.

She lay there in the driveway, praying one of the neighbors would call the police. In her heart she knew that wouldn't happen. It never did. The whole neighborhood was terrified of her father. She tried to move once more, but her strength was gone in waves of pain.

Suddenly the pain was gone. A vast presence surrounded her, soothing her, and holding the pain at bay. "Who or what are you?" she asked silently. "How are you doing this?"

"How does not matter, Lenora, my child," said a gentle yet rich and loving voice. It spoke only in her mind, responding to the questions she thought of, but was unable to utter. *"What matters is, you are badly injured. I can heal you, if you so desire."*

"Go for it," thought Lenora. "I know you want something, and I'll do it whatever it is. Just get me away from here."

"I do have a task for you, Lenora, however, that can wait until you're rested and healed. For the moment, I will heal your injuries if you promise to listen fully to my proposal afterwards. Once you can make a decision not based on pain, we'll talk. For now, I will heal you if you promise to listen."

"I'll listen to anything as long as I survive. Please get me away from here before he comes out after me."

"He will not harm you further, I promise. Be still now and I will heal you."

Lenora sighed as a wave of sweet loving energy swept through her. She giggled as she felt her ribs and arm shift back into place and knit together. She almost shouted with glee as her energy soared. Her teeth stopped hurting and moved back into place, and then her eyes opened again. She was alone in the driveway. She could still feel the vast loving presence surrounding her, but she was alone.

With a cry of delight, she surged to her feet and sprinted away as the door banged open behind her. She heard her father swearing as he gave chase, but she shouted with glee as she sped on.

Lenora felt she could run forever. She fairly flew down the street, across the open field and down to the river. Reaching the bridge she looked back. Her tormentor had long since given up the race. Lenora fairly danced down the embankment and hid herself from sight. She could still feel the presence with her.

"Okay, I'm like the troll under the bridge now," she said, as she sat on a rock beside the sluggish river. "I think I'm safe enough to talk. Who are you and how can I ever repay you for what you've done?"

"I am Moragah, goddess of Wisdom and Defender of the Weak. From time to time I create a priestess to serve me in special ways. I was looking for just such a person when I found you.

"A priestess? Serve you in special ways?"

There was amusement in Moragah's voice now and it made Lenora smile. She felt so safe and loved in the presence of the goddess. *"It isn't quite as you might imagine. I am familiar with modern religions, but they do not resemble what I need from you in any way. Permit me to show you some of the other priestesses."*

It was like watching a movie. Lenora saw a blonde girl fairly flying across the rooftops to drop like a bomb into a street gang. She watched as the girl demolished the aggressors. Next was a dark girl with cold deadly eyes. She stepped out of a wall and destroyed several men who were beating a woman. Next was a small blonde who threw fire from her hands then walked through it to carry a victim away from abusers. The last was an elvish warrior riding on the back of a dragon. When the beast landed she morphed into a woman not much older than Lenora.

"Wow," she breathed. "They're amazing."

"Penny fights brutality wherever she finds it. Kara and Tasha fight to bring justice back to a city that has seen too little of it. And Lady Shadow, Seline, is a hunter. She hunts the bringers of darkness and stops them. She strives to return the balance between the darkness and the light."

"You want to make me like them?"

"*Yes and no, Lenora. I have a different task for you, if you are willing to undertake it.*"

"No dragons. I'm afraid of heights. I'd fall off that monster and break my neck."

Moragah's delight filled her and she couldn't repress a giggle. "*Very well, no dragons for you. No, Lenora, I have given Seline great power for her task is the greatest of them all. For you, I would give you different abilities. You would be stronger than a dozen men. Your injuries would heal almost instantly. When attacked or under stress you would shift onto combat mode wherein you move at incredible speed and everything else seems to be in slow motion.*

"*I need a seeker, Lenora. So many souls and more are lost and abandoned in this world. So many have no resource, yet, unknown to them there are those who love them and search for them constantly. Your task would be to find the lost, both human and other, and reunite them with the ones who love them. For this task you would have the ability to track by scent like a hunting wolf. You would be able to see in the dark, climb easily when it seems impossible to climb, and you would instinctively avoid danger. You would also have a built in sense of direction. These attributes and more will be yours if you will help me.*"

"All that and more? And I get to help reunite others with their families? But what if their family is like mine?"

"*You would know instantly, Lenora, and would refuse to aid the family. Remember, defend the weak is our main motive.*"

"Moragah, I feel better right now than I have ever felt before. I'll do it. Oh god, I can't wait to get started."

"*There is one more thing.*"

"Oh?"

"*Yes. Once we do this there is no turning back, ever. You will be mine completely. My laws and only my laws will pertain to you. I will possess you and always be with you, experiencing everything you experience. I will always be with you as a part of you. Also, Whenever possible, I would enjoy a prayer of greeting at sunrise each day. Is this acceptable to you?"*

Lenora didn't hesitate. "Got it. I can do this, and having you as a living part of me would be wonderful beyond anything I have ever experienced."

"Then you are mine, my daughter. Brace yourself for I am told this hurts like hellfire, but it only lasts a moment. And then I will sooth your pain and you will be Lady Seeker."

Lenora took a deep breath then nodded. Suddenly every cell in her body seemed to burst into flame ripping a blood curdling scream from her lips. The pain was gone before the sound of her scream died on the air. She sat, hand over her heart, breathing deeply.

"It is done, Lady Seeker, my priestess. Be ready, for your abuser approaches even now."

"Oh crap, he'll find me. What am I going to do?"

"What you must, my priestess. I have prepared you. Deal with this man as you see fit."

"I'd like to kill him."

"Then do so with my blessing." So saying, Moragah pulled back and Lenora was alone beneath the bridge, standing on the gravel bar as her father came down the bank and rushed at her.

Suddenly his world went all to hell. She kicked him and broke his leg. She then leaped at him and broke one of his arms.

With one hand she gripped his throat and held him up in the air. "Never again, you hear me, never again. If I ever hear of you hitting my mother again I'll come back and beat you to death. Understand?" She dropped him then walked away, crossing the river on exposed stones, and disappearing up the opposite bank. She didn't even go back for her car.

Don't miss out!

Visit the website below and you can sign up to receive emails whenever Prudence MacLeod publishes a new book. There's no charge and no obligation.

https://books2read.com/r/B-A-ZKBBB-MIMTC

BOOKS 2 READ

Connecting independent readers to independent writers.

Also by Prudence MacLeod

Children of the Goddess
Lady Blue
Fallen Angel
Lady Justice
Lady Shadow

Forgotten Worlds
Suvi
Echo of the Past
Survivors
Ship
Fleet
Unite
IGEN
T.E.N.

Nova series
Novan Witch
Assassin of Nova
Beyond Nova

Claimstake
Red Nova

Watch for more at https://www.prudencemacleod.com/.

About the Author

Jennifer Crandall writes and publishes under three different names, Prudence MacLeod, J.L.Crandall, and Jenni Leigh. Learn more about her on her website,

Read more at https://www.prudencemacleod.com/.